The Honeyed Taste of Deception

by CeeCee James

Table of Contents

Chapter 1

"911...what's your emergency?"

The operator's voice did little to pry Elise from her shock. All she could see was the frosting—pink, green and white—with nonpareils spilling from a bottle into a pile beside the dead body. Resting next to the corpse's foot was a very conspicuous, fake, red nose.

"Uhh... there...there's..." Elise stammered. Her ears rang as the blood rushed from her face. Dizzily, she reached for the table to steady herself. She flinched as her fingers dug into more frosting.

"What's your emergency?" The calm voice asked again.

Elise's mouth was dry as she tried to croak out the words. "Something's happened to the cake decorator."

"Can you give me some more details? Is his airway clear?"

"Um, I think he's dead."

"Are you sure he's deceased?" The voice was irritating in its calmness.

Elise straightened her shoulders as she got a grip on the situation. "Quite sure. He's been shot in the heart."

❈ ❈ ❈

Two weeks earlier

❈ ❈ ❈

Lavina and Elise sat at a bistro table outside Sweet Sandwiches Deli. The establishment was Lavina's baby and, as such, she examined the exterior seating arrangements with a critical eye to make sure everything was perfectly placed before she relaxed with her mug of tea. The aroma of the steam rising from their mugs was thick with the scent of cinnamon, and both women breathed in deeply. Although spring was on the calendar, it definitely wasn't in the Tennessee air, as evidenced by Elise shivering in her cardigan.

"Why are we sitting out here again?" Elise asked, burying her nose in the top of her sweater, her hands clasped tightly around the warm mug.

"My doctor told me to get more vitamin D," Lavina said, pulling out her cell phone from her Dooney & Bourke purse.

Elise eyed her best friend swathed in a wooly scarf and a thick Persian shawl. "What part of your skin is getting the vitamin D exactly?"

Lavina looked up, eyes covered with a pair of overly-large rhinestone-encrusted sunglasses. "You hush, now. It's getting on my face."

Elise raised an eyebrow and burrowed further into her cardigan. "I can hardly believe you lack any vitamin D with all those exotic vacations you're constantly taking with Mr. G."

With a flicker of her well-plucked eyebrow, Lavina joked back. "You know we don't leave the room too much."

"Weird. I don't need to hear this. Please."

Lavina laughed. "Speaking of Mr. G, he's picking me up in," she glanced at her phone for the time. "Twenty minutes."

Well, this was something new. A chance to actually clap eyes on Lavina's mysterious boyfriend. All Elise knew about him was that he was extremely rich and topped Lavina's own thirty-four years by another thirty.

"Will you look at this?" Lavina shoved her phone over. Stretched across the screen in big letters was the statement, **Jewel Thief Strikes Again.** "That's the third time since winter started."

Elise glanced at the article briefly, barely taking in the details of the jewelry store robberies. Granted, she was distracted. Her mind was still spinning over the idea of meeting Mr. G after all these years. Suddenly, she sat upright. "He'll be here in twenty minutes you say?"

"Darlin', what's wrong with you?" Lavina's perfectly manicured hand tucked the cell phone back into her designer bag. "I just said that."

Elise had bad feeling. "What time is it?"

"Just a little after eleven thirty."

Crap. Elise gathered her stuff together and stuffed it into her bag. She took another sip from her mug. "I'm sorry. I have to go."

Lavina looked puzzled before a knowing look crossed her face. She relaxed with understanding. "Oh, that's right. You have a job," she said drolly.

"I hope I have a job. I've got to get there right now." Elise stood up from the table and gave Lavina a hug, cursing her luck that she was going to miss a chance to finally meet the infamous Mr. G. *Can't be helped. Not if I want to eat this month.* Sighing, she ran for her car.

Her little Pinto wasn't much, but she was thankful for it. The car's ignition whined a few times as she turned the key. Pumping the gas, she whispered encouragingly, "Come on, hot stuff. Come on..."

Finally, the car roared to life and she smiled triumphantly. Well, roared might be a slight exaggeration. She shifted the car into drive and drove the Pinto to the exit of the parking lot, wincing a little as it backfired.

Crossing in front of her was a group of kids wearing t-shirts with the logo of the local daycare center, probably on their way to the park. The children laughed and spun in front of her car while she impatiently tapped the steering wheel. *Cute, you guys are so cute. But hurry up!* She glanced at the dash clock and groaned. Her first day on the job and it looked like she'd be late. Finally, a daycare worker rounded up the caboose—a freckled boy—and the road was clear.

She drove anxiously through town, looking for the bridal shop. It still amused her that she of all people, jaded from a fresh divorce from a cheating ex-husband, would be helping nauseatingly in-love people finalize their own marriages, but a job was a job. Besides, she had to admit, the idea of being a part of making someone's dream come true intrigued her.

After all, the name of the shop was Wedding Dreams, and there it was, looking just as pink and frilly as it possibly could from the exterior. Elise shoe-horned the Pinto into the remaining spot in front of the building and climbed out. The boutique's front display window was layered in tulle and white satin. Sitting in the center of the fabric was a fake five layer wedding cake—roses and all—on a crystal stand. A glittery sign hung above it with gold letters spelling out, "Making your wedding dreams come true since 2008."

The sign on the door read, "Closed," stabbing Elise with a sharp needle of worry as she reached for the doorknob. But the door opened with a sweet bell tinkle. The inside of the boutique was full-blown pink, with white couches covered in fluffy cushions. Giant, gilt framed mirrors replicated and tripled the room's interior over and over.

Elise looked around for the owner. She'd spoken with her several times over the last week. On the phone, the voice had sounded stern but sweet, and Elise imagined the owner to be a small woman with short brown hair. A kind soul whose job was to comfort the poor brides-to-be, but who also had nerves of steel to navigate a wedding's choppy waters. Maybe tiny eyes behind thick spectacles and a button-up cardigan, really a librarian type.

The boutique appeared empty. Elise glanced beyond the couches toward the silky curtains that partitioned off the room. There was no one who matched that description. In fact, no one at all.

"Hello?" Elise called, feeling a bit trepidatious. She glanced at her watch and frowned. *Shoot, ten minutes late.* She cleaned her throat and called out louder. "Hello? Anybody here?"

"Be right there!" The sweet, melodious voice sang out from behind the curtain. There was rustling, and then loud clumping heralded a hand pushing back the curtain.

Elise felt her jaw drop at the sight of the woman. She quickly closed it and pasted on a big smile. *This couldn't be her? Could it?*

Any doubt Elise had was shrugged off as the woman walked forward, combat boots thumping loudly despite the thick carpet, with her hand outstretched.

"I'm Sonya, the owner here at Dreams boutique," the soft voice greeted her, shaking Elise from her shock.

"H..hi." Elise recovered and shook Sonya's hand. The strong grip made Elise's eyebrows ratchet up in alarm. Carefully, Elise extricated her hand from the knuckle-popping grip of the other woman.

Sonya stood nearly six feet tall, and was tattooed from head to toe. At least, every square inch of skin that Elise could see was covered in ink.

Stars dotted the back of Sonya's arm, trailing up before melding into an intricate sleeve of flowers and birds. Surprisingly, her face was free from makeup under a shock of bleached white hair.

"Not what you were expecting?" Again, the soft voice threw Elise a curveball. Elise struggled to keep her face from displaying her confusion as she smiled.

Sonya continued, "I throw on a sweater when I'm with customers. Besides, they aren't paying for how I look, but for what I can do for them." She raised an eyebrow. "And believe me, no one is better at what I do."

Elise nodded, feeling the woman's confidence. This woman was no-nonsense and looked like she got what she wanted. "I'm Elise. It's nice to meet you." Elise made a show of looking around the room. "It's certainly is amazing in here!"

"You may want to withhold judgement on whether it's nice to meet me." Sonya said, her eyebrow raised.

"I've been told I'm a beast to work with. My last assistant quit without any warning."

Elise swallowed and smiled again.

Taking a few steps toward the back of the room, Sonya reached for a thick binder that had been resting on a buffet. She flipped it open and ran her finger down the paper. "Right now, I'm working with two brides-to-be. The first one is getting married this weekend, and so we're working under fire right now. I'm basically throwing you to the wolves this week, and it's up to you to prove whether you can handle it. I don't have time to baby you. I never babysit." Sonya's soft voice was the antithesis of the words she used. "This business is stress multiplying stress. Like I told you on the phone, it's dealing with emotional women and their histrionics. Some stuff can't be taught but must come from the grit inside." Here, Sonya clenched her fist, making her tattoos jump, and hit herself in the chest. "You think you've got grit?"

Elise nodded and licked her lips nervously.

"The second bride-to-be doesn't hit her date until mid-September," Sonya continued.

Elise nodded again, noting the six month time difference.

"She's been here once before, and she's coming for another consultation again today." Sonya snapped the case closed over the tablet and gave Elise a hard stare. "I'm warning you now, she's a head case. That little Miss Priss has been making me work harder than I've ever worked." Sonya glanced at the front door and grabbed a pink cardigan off the back of a chair, quickly slipping it on. "And speaking of the bride-to-be, here she is now."

Chapter 2

The boutique's front door opened to reveal a blonde, petite woman in one of the tallest, most sparkling pairs of stiletto shoes Elise had ever seen. And that was saying a lot since Lavina seemed to live in high heels—even wearing them to the beach.

"Hello! Hello!" The bride-to-be's voice was high-pitched and chipper like a bird's. She tottered in with her hair piled in curls on top of her head.

On her right, with his hand hovering near her elbow, in case the tiny woman should fall, was a tall man with a shock of red hair. He nodded good-naturedly as the blonde woman reached out a hand to Elise. "Rhonda! My name is Catalina! I'm so happy to meet you after all of our phone conversations. It's just crazy to be here. A dream finally coming true!"

Elise took Catalina's hand awkwardly, waiting for a pause in the stream of words so she could correct the mistaken identity, but Catalina was not to be deterred. Swiveling around on one silver heel, the blonde-haired woman continued. "This place is ah-mazing! Just like a fairy-tale." Her blue eyes opened wide to take in the boutique. With a giggle, she flashed her gaze back at Elise. "I can definitely tell that I'm in capable hands! Are you ready to hear some more about all of my dreams?"

At that moment, Sonya cut in with her manly hand outstretched. "Hello, Catalina. This is my new assistant, Elise. Rhonda, with whom you've spoken with on the phone, unexpectedly left last week. Welcome back to Wedding Dreams."

Catalina blinked in confusion before disengaging her hand from Elise's. She took Sonya's with a bit less enthusiasm, as if trying to decide if she was being punked. Seeming to decide that she was not, Catalina's face blossomed into full joy again. "Oh, my! I was so silly to assume. Who would have thought this job would have a big over-turn? It's nice to see *you* again, at any rate."

"No worries at all. I'm doing great and glad to be of service for your wonderful day. Now, I haven't met you yet." Sonya glanced up at the man, her expression transforming to look matronly, with her eyebrows raised in question.

"Name's Cook Faraday," the man answered and reached out to shake Sonya's hand. "I guess I'm the one footing the bill."

"Oh, Cook," Catalina squealed. "You know I'm worth it. It's about time you made me an honest woman."

"Come, have a seat in my lounge and let's hear more about your thoughts for your big day." Sonya smiled. "Can I get you a glass of champagne?" Despite her heavy boots, Sonya turned and glided toward the pink door at the back of the boutique. Catalina giggled continuously as she reached for Cook's arm. Elise trailed behind the group, feeling slightly at a loss as to what to do.

The four of them moved into Sonya's consultation room. Elise's head swiveled around taking everything in just the same as the bride and groom.

"Here, make yourself comfortable." Sonya gestured toward two white leather chairs that were situated before a glass desk. In the corner of the room, a crystal vase overflowed with white roses, chrysanthemums and lilies. The floral arrangement filled the small room with a heady scent.

Sonya walked to the sideboard and retrieved the champagne from the ice bucket and brought it to her desk. She then returned to gather the fluted glasses, setting them next to the bottle with a clink. Facing the wall with a look of concentration, Sonya slowly began to push on the cork on the bottle.

Elise held her breath as she waited for the cork to pop.

POP!

All four of them jumped and then laughed at the sound. Sonya tipped the bottle and poured the bubbly amber liquid into the glasses. The champagne lightly fizzed as she passed them out.

"Elise?" Sonya asked, tipping her head to an extra glass on the buffet. Elise shook her head, no, and Sonya nodded.

"So," Sonya said as she settled in her chair across from the bride and groom and wove her fingers in front of her thoughtfully. "Tell me what you're dreaming of, and I'll tell you how I can make it happen."

Catalina giggled and took a sip from her glass. Her fiancé, smiled at her with a look of indulgence. "I'm kind of all over the board right now since our last talk."

"Oh? What's changed?" Sonya's eyebrows flickered.

"I think I need a miracle. We need to get married in two weeks." Catalina twirled a bracelet around her wrist, seeming to not want to make eye contact.

Sonya's pale lips pressed together and even her normally soft voice was affected. "Two. Weeks. You can't be serious. I wouldn't even be able to guarantee that I could get you in front of a Justice of the Peace to elope in that time."

Cook cleared his voice. "Unfortunately, I'm shipping out then."

"Oh?" Sonya looked at him in confusion. His red hair was on the longish side and not cut in the normal military high-and-tight. He noticed her glance and ran his hand through his hair.

"I'm a contractor," he explained. "I'm needed overseas at the end of next month to fulfill a few of my contracts."

"I know it's impossible, but I guess that's the start of my dream," Catalina said finally looking up, her big blue eyes staring wide.

Sonya nodded, biting her bottom lip. She unclasped her hands and tapped her nails against the desk's surface. "If I did this, it would have to be the simplest wedding I've ever planned. Nothing extravagant. I won't be able to do it in a big hall."

"Oh, no. No!" Catalina exclaimed. "We actually want to have it outdoors. In that big park over in Eddington.

Sonya shook her head. "Don't get your hopes up about a park wedding. I'm not sure the city would grant us a permit in this little amount of time."

"Please. Is there any way at all? Can you try?" Catalina sniffled then and, looking pitiful, rummaged in her oversized purse. Elise expected her to pull out a tissue, but instead she removed a battered photograph. Catalina smiled at it before pushing it across the desk.

"There's one more reason. My family will be in town then. This is my daddy. He's...." her voice cracked. "He's not doing well." Cook patted his fiancé's arm and Catalina rested her head against his shoulder with her eyes squeezed tight.

Leaning forward, Elise could just make out an old man in the picture before Sonya picked it up. The wedding planner studied it closely before handing it back with a small nod. "I'll see what I can do. But don't hold your breath, okay? You might just end up getting married right in here if we can't get things squared away in two weeks."

A smile broke out across Catalina's face and her eyes shone with happiness. "Thank you so much!" Like a child, she clapped her hands together.

Elise blew out a breath of air she hadn't realized she'd been holding. Talk about being out of the frying pan and into the fire. Two weddings in two weeks? This just seemed to be a disaster in the making.

Catalina tucked the picture back into her purse. Elise couldn't help but wonder why her all of family would be in town. Seemed convenient. Was poor

Catalina's father's death that imminent? Why have a wedding at all then?

BOOM!

A loud bang from outside startled the four of them. When it happened again, Sonya jumped up and raced for the entrance door.

Chapter 3

The four of them elbowed for room around the boutique's display window.

"What was that noise?" Catalina asked in a breathless voice. Cook hovered protectively around her.

"I don't know, but there's a siren now." Elise responded, her heart pounding.

"I think it's coming from the jewelry store," Sonya murmured, her forehead creased. She moved away from the window and reached for the door. The three others followed her as she threw it open.

Sure enough, Grandstone Jewels rattled its alarm. People fled the building like a stream of trout, panic on their faces. But what struck Elise as bizarre were all the painters milling around the jewelry store's entrance.

Painters?

Clad in white coveralls and hats, most even had particle masks over their mouths or hanging by the straps around their necks. A white van was parked against the curb.

Masks.

"Shut the door." Elise said as premonition tickled the back of her neck. Sonya didn't respond, frozen with concentration.

Elise touched the owner's arm to get her attention. "Hurry, shut the door."

"Will you stop? I'm trying to see what's going on." Sonya jerked her arm away and leaned out farther. Cold air swirled along the floor.

Another quick glance outside showed Elise that some of the painters now faced their direction, their eyes dark over the tops of the white masks.

"Oh, sweet heavens," Elise hissed. "Now, Sonya!"

Sonya's eyes widened and she slammed the door shut and locked it tight. The three women, along with Cook, crowded back around the display window of the boutique. Catalina pushed the taffeta away from the wedding cake display and climbed up on the stage.

Elise watched silently. All four of them were quiet, actually, trying to make out what was happening outside. She still couldn't understand it. The painters weren't acting like she'd expect. Why weren't they running? Didn't they just rob the jewelry store?

Instead, although the alarm continued to wail, the painters stumbled about looking very disassociated. Some buckled together in a group. A few lowered their dust masks and talked to one another with arms waving.

"What in the world is going on?" The words dropped slowly from Elise's mouth. Finally, a police car arrived with its lights flashing. Red and blue splashed across the painter's faces and white coveralls.

More police cars arrive and soon Grandstone Jewels was surrounded by officers. The painters were cordoned in a group to one side, the customers on the other. Both groups were slowly interviewed.

Yellow tape was draped about like May-Day ribbons. One by one, both the customers and painters drifted away.

The three women and Cook watched all of this in shocked silence. Finally, Sonya pushed off the display case as the last painter walked away. "Well, you don't see that every day."

"They just let them go," Catalina murmured. "The cops just let those painters go."

"It must have been a coincidence they were there," Cook answered, looking confused as well. He rubbed the back of his neck with his brow furrowed.

"Well, I don't know about you, but I could use some champagne," Sonya announced as she stalked back to the conference room.

Catalina and Cook followed, looking like half-deflated hot-air balloons. The excited energy was gone, replaced by uncertainty and adrenaline fatigue.

Elise watched out the window some more. Most of the officers were inside the building now. A stray piece of yellow tape fluttered in the wind. She shook her head with her own confusion, and turned to join the other three.

❖ ❖ ❖

The next few days passed in a blur for Elise. Sonya was a demanding boss, every bit as hard as she'd warned that first day. Elise found herself constantly on the run, either literally or coaxing her Pinto around town, as the boutique prepared for the first wedding.

But, as crazy as the preparations was, it was a crash course in wedding planning too. Each morning began with a long note from the owner—Sonya still worked off of paper lists—filled from top to bottom with the day's assignments. In just those two days, Elise familiarized herself with the boutique's favorite hairdresser, dry cleaner, bakery chef, and florist.

Each night, Elise collapsed on the couch, exhausted. In fact, after a particularly grueling day trying to locate a missing veil, she'd gone to straight to bed still dressed in her work clothes.

Tonight was no different. It was supposed to be a date night, and Brad's car was in the driveway when she pulled up. They'd been seeing each other pretty steady for the last few months, and had just swapped house keys with each other.

She stumbled in through the door, so thankful he was there.

"Hey, gorgeous," Brad greeted from the kitchen. He peeked his head out the doorway, his dark hair tousled. "Wow, you look wiped out."

Elise half-laughed and rubbed her cheeks, hoping to bring color to them. She could only imagine the zombie state she must look like, considering how she felt.

"I mean," he amended, his green eyes crinkling at the corners with a gentle smile, "it's a beautiful tired. You eat anything?"

She glanced at the clock—ten pm—before shaking her head no, too tired to speak. She flopped down on the couch and rested her head against the back. Her cat, a beautiful orange tabby she'd rescued named Max, jumped beside her. She stroked his foot with one finger.

"Aww, you poor baby. Let me dish you up some food." Brad said, disappearing back in the kitchen.

Elise rolled her head to the side toward the TV. The news was on, her least favorite show. Her fingers slowly scrabbled across the couch cushion for the remote but it was just out of reach. Too tired to care, she closed her eyes.

"Thank you for joining us for the ten o'clock news. Tonight, we bring you the latest information on the jewelry store robbery that occurred earlier this week in Angel Lake. Police finally feel that they have evidence that links this robbery to others that have been happening around the state since Thanksgiving, including the last one in Meadowford."

Elise opened her eyes and straightened up.

"In a bizarre twist, the police have located an ad posted to Craigslist promoting a house painting service. The ad reads, and I quote, 'everyone who shows up in painter's gear, ready to go, will be hired.' According to jewelry store witnesses, the robber also wore painter's gear and may have disappeared in the crowd of painters waiting outside."

Elise paused the TV. "Brad, did you see this?" she called toward the kitchen where plastic could be heard crinkling.

The plastic bag rattling escalated, followed by a rip and then the patter of a thousand flimsy things hitting the floor at once. Silence followed. Max jumped from the couch and, after licking his back a few times as though disinterested, sauntered into the kitchen to investigate.

"Brad," Elise asked cautiously. "Do you need help?"

"Everything's fine in here," came the answer, laced with sarcasm.

Elise nodded and tossed the remote to the coffee table before standing up. Every muscle screamed. "What's going on in there?" She walked to the kitchen and peeked around the entryway.

Brad was standing in a sea of potato chips, a sandwich before him on a plate. Max sniffed at one before batting it with his paws. As soon as the chip moved the game was on, with Max swatting it again and chasing after the skittering chip.

Brad held out the offending chip bag, now torn length-ways down its side. "It wouldn't open," he explained. "I was looking for a snack for myself."

She couldn't help the laugh that bubbled up at his cute look. "No worries. I have—Max! Stop that!—I have some popcorn."

Brad dropped to his knees to gather the chips, grumbling, "No one can eat just one, unless they have cat hair all over them."

"Ew!" Elise stooped to help him. "My floor's clean. The top layer of chips is probably fine."

He popped one into his mouth and crunched. "Not bad."

Elise swept the pile into the bowl that had been waiting for them. "Anyway. Did you hear about that jewelry store robbery? It's on the news right now and they're calling them the Craigslist Bandits."

"Oh, they're releasing that information now, huh?" He stood up and brushed his hand on his pants.

Elise threw a dishtowel at him on her way to the pantry.

"Yeah," her voice was muffled as she searched for her popcorn amidst the crowded shelves. "So you already know? Aha!" Holding the microwave popcorn triumphantly, she shut the door and turned.

Brad had crossed his arms and was leaning against the counter. His eyebrow lowered over one eye as he gave her a cocky grin. "It's this weird thing about

31

being a cop. I kind of know how an investigation is going."

"Whatever, smart-aleck. I didn't know if this robbery in town was for sure connected to the ones across the state." She opened the cellophane bag and placed the popcorn in the microwave.

"Sorry. We just confirmed it last night," Brad said.

"The Craigslist angle is pretty wild, huh? It's kind of cool."

"Yeah, it's been interesting. Usually, we get the dumb as a cockroach criminals, but this one actually put some thought into it."

"How did you find out about the ad?"

"Just interviewing the painters. All those workers had responded to an ad that said, show up at noon at this parking lot, dressed in full gear. And boom, there they were."

"So there were ads connected to the other robberies?"

He nodded. "Yeah. One was a flash dance mob, and the other a group of protestors."

"A dance mob? You're kidding me! What was the dance?"

"Can't Catch Me." Brad's lip quirked up at the corner. "Apparently, the robbers are a little arrogant."

"And what was the protesting about?"

"A rally to raise minimum wage."

"Mmm," Elise said. "And at a jewelry store. Spread the wealth."

"We seem to have robbers well-versed in the art of irony."

"But this one has painters. That doesn't seem as similar." She stood on her tip-toes and grabbed a bowl from the top shelf.

"The ad was for Bandit Painting Services."

Elise laughed and nearly dropped the bowl. "You're kidding me. That's hilarious."

"Hilarious or not, we're talking about someone's property."

"It's all insured though, right?"

Brad narrowed his eyes. "Don't tell me you're falling for the whole Robin Hood aspect of this. Just because there's insurance doesn't mean it's okay to just take it."

"Oh, I know. I'm not thinking Robin Hood. I was really scared to the bone when I heard that alarm go off and saw all those painters standing out there."

She retrieved the popcorn and poured it into the bowl, shaking the bag to get out the last few pieces.

"There's nothing harmless about entering a room full of people and saying it's an armed robbery." Brad refilled his glass from the sink.

Her mouth dropped open. "They had guns?"

"No one has verified them yet, but, yeah, they threaten to use weapons. I'm not sure why they haven't flaunted them during the robbery. Maybe they keep them under wraps because they know jewelry stores have protocol to comply with demands like that."

Elise grabbed her sandwich and kissed him. "Thank you, sweetheart." The two returned to the living room and settled back into the couch.

On the TV screen, the reporter's mouth was still frozen in mid-sentence about the Craigslist Bandits. Brad placed his cup on the table as Elise set the popcorn bowl between them on a cushion.

"Protocol, huh? Do you think the robbers work in a jewelry store?" Elise took a bite of the sandwich. Mmm, turkey and lettuce, one of her favorites. Chewing, she sighed with contentment.

"Not sure. It's one possibility we're looking at."

"Maybe a disgruntled employee?"

Brad snorted. "No, we're looking more into debts, who just incurred a debt, who might need money to get out of debt. Believe it or not, credit scores can really help."

"You can just get someone's credit score without their permission?"

"They give their permission when they get hired on at the jewelry store."

Elise's phone vibrated. She pulled it free from her pocket.

It was a text from Sonya.

9 am sharp. See you at the church.

Chapter 4

A quarter to eight found Elise driving through the outskirts of town searching for the church. Two more turns and finally the church's steeple came into sight. The fleet of cars already parked in the lot was reassuring, but Elise double checked her directions anyway. Yep. This was where the wedding was at.

She pulled around the back side of the building and found a spot to park. Then, after gathering her duffle and sweater, she ran for the entrance, passing Sonya's VW bus on the way in.

I'm not late. Don't stress. Still, her pulse raced as she flew up the concrete steps and opened the big oak doors.

Inside, the chaos and noise was like nothing Elise had ever seen.

Someone shouted to her left, and she ducked out of the way of a man carrying an armload of roses. Straightening her shoulders, Elise took a big breath and walked toward the sanctuary.

Sonya was in the center of a human foray, waving black taffeta covered arms in a series of directions. Elise was amazed at the proprietor's transformation, from tough biker woman to a vision of elegance in her high heels and fitted pencil skirt. Elise brushed down her own skirt and hurried over.

Sonya lifted her soft voice so that it carried over the crowd to a pair of men holding two green floral arrangements. "Toward the altar please, with those. Careful!"

The men grunted as they carried the huge planters. With a look of worry, Sonya watched after them a moment before she caught a glimpse of Elise. "Oh! There you are!"

"I'm sorry. I thought you said to be here at nine."

Sonya's lips tightened. "I just assumed you'd understand that we need to be here as soon as possible to get things ready. We want everything perfect, and it takes eyes and bodies to make sure that happens."

Flustered, Elise nodded and clasped her hands before her. "What would you like me to do?"

Sonya flipped through her sheath of papers before passing over a stack. "Go to The Farm's banquet hall. Make sure it's all set up like it's supposed to be. And check on the flower deliveries. Darrel!" Sonya interrupted herself to address a harried looking man rushing by. "Did you call the catering company?"

The dark-haired man held his hands up as if to ward her off as fear came into his eyes. "No, I'm sorry. I've been chasing down the pastry chef to make sure he had the new cake topper."

"When I give you a job to do..." Sonya warned.

"I'm sorry! I'll call him right now."

Her gray eyes narrowed. "Forget it. You're fired." She turned to Elise and once more rifled through the paperwork in her hands. Pulling out another sheet, she handed it over. "Call the catering company too, and make sure everything is as scheduled."

Darrel stood with his eyes wide with shock. "Are you serious right now? You can't just fire me!"

"I just did," Sonya deadpanned. She turned on the toe of her shoe and marched across the room.

Darrel watched her, slack jawed. Finally, he flipped her off and hurried for the door. One of the female assistants who stood watching sidled up to Elise. "Let me give you a piece of advice. Always come two hours before she asks. It's when she shows up, and she expects everyone else to do likewise." The girl tapped the papers in Elise's hands. "And I'd hurry to get this done if I were you."

❊ ❊ ❊

Elise drove another ten minutes in the opposite direction, on her way to the Farm Banquet Hall. She thought about Sonya. *That woman is so hard. Is that what it takes to own a business like this? How long has she owned Wedding Dreams? I've always wanted to own my own business, but not if it takes that kind of attitude.*

She turned up the radio, smiling as she caught the end of her favorite song. *I need to make time to run again. Probably help my stress a ton.*

The next street led to Angel Lake's central park. The Farm Banquet Hall butted up against a grassy knoll of the park and was gorgeous with its landscaping. Lattice arches covered with purple wisteria led to the main entryway.

Elise had loved this place as a little girl. Both she and Lavina had picked the fallen wisteria blossoms every year and hung them to dry in their bedroom windows. They'd sworn at the time that crumbling the dried flowers on their pillows at night would bring them dreams of their future husbands. She smiled as she parked the car.

As Elise walked up the sidewalk to the hall's entrance, a man loped up from the opposite direction. His reek of alcohol hit her and her first response was to shy away.

"Excuse me," His voice was polite and he raised his hand to stop her. "Miss, do you have a dollar?"

She glanced up at the hall before shaking her head. "All I have is change," she added, reaching into her pocket. His hand shook as she spilled the coins into his dirty palm.

"Thank you so much. Now, how about if I give you something?" He squinted, his jaw dark with whiskers.

"Back away, buddy," Elise warned, tightening her fist. She clutched her purse and papers closer to her chest and continued to walk toward the entrance.

He laughed, but it sounded sad. "I just wanted to let you know the circus is in town." He patted his chest, a flannel shirt covering a torn t-shirt. "That's where I'm from. Or was. Before last night."

Elise's hand was on the door when she finally turned back. "I'm sorry you lost your job."

"My job?" He snorted and shook his head, greasy hair falling into his eyes. "No. No, I still have my job."

Still has his job? What is he begging for then? "All right, well, thank you for letting me know." Elise said as she opened the door.

"You should check it out. Best circus this side of the Rockies." He thumped his chest proudly again with the hand that still held the coins. "Worked there for ten years."

Elise paused. "Why'd they let you go?"

He shook his head. "Like I said, I have a job to do. And it's going to pay me real well." He raised his hand to say goodbye and continued to shamble down the sidewalk.

Well, that was weird. Elise lifted her eyebrows in disbelief and walked inside.

The inside of the banquet hall was a replica of the same frenetic activity that she'd left at the church. *These people look like starving chickens after a crop of grasshoppers.* Elise danced to the left to avoid a man carrying a ladder. She looked around for someone in charge.

It appeared to be no one. A woman rifling through cards at a table across the room glanced up and caught her eye. After scooping up the cards, the woman rushed over. "Thank goodness you're here! We've been waiting all morning for someone to show up," she said. The papers slipped through her hands and ruffled into the air like the biggest game of 52 card pickup in the world.

Oh. Apparently it's me. Elise's thoughts dripped with sarcasm as she turned up the confident smile to greet the woman. "Hi, there. I'm just here to check that everything is on schedule. How are things looking?"

The woman scowled at the cards and dropped to her knees to scoop them up. Elise squatted to help her, no easy task in heels and a skirt.

"My name's Tanya," the woman said. "Sonya said you'd be on your way."

Elise held out her own lists and said, "Okay, let's get this done. How much time do we have?"

Tanya glanced at her watch. "Five hours. I have some good news and some bad news."

The two women stood up. Elise steeled herself. "Okay, hit me with the bad news."

After taking a deep breath, Tanya spouted the words in a rush, "The cake is missing, the florist brought the wrong flowers, the chef forgot to plan a gluten-free alternative for the bride's mom, and half the champagne bottles broke in transit. Oh, and the DJ says he absolutely won't work unless the strobe light is on at all times."

Elise felt herself blanch. "What's the good news?"

Tanya smiled brightly. "We found the wedding cake topper."

❋❋❋

The two women worked like dogs all morning. The chef was notified of the alternative menu items he needed to provide and had rectified the situation. The cake had been located and set up under Elise's watchful eye.

The wrong flowers couldn't be fixed but the florist was able to use them as filler with the correct flowers. The DJ was soothed with a bottle of brandy, and a clerk was sent out for more champagne.

All in all, Elise thought things were coming together nicely. In fact, the most interesting thing all morning was the chatter about the Craigslist Bandits. A week passing had only added fuel to the gossip chain in this small town. People were scouring Craigslist hoping to find another suspicious ad. Grandstone Jewelers had made a generous offer of ten thousand dollars for any information.

"Ladies and gentlemen, how are things looking?" Sonya's melodious voice cut through the small talk as she strode across the room. Elise turned to search for her. Ah, there she was, but what was she carrying? In her hand was a half-used toilet paper roll, the end fluttering with her boss's steps. "Elise!" Sonya called when she caught her eye. "I sent you to make sure everything is perfect. What is this?"

"Uhh?" Elise wasn't sure how to respond.

"A nearly empty roll of toilet paper in the bride's changing room? No, it's details like these that make my blood boil. Brand new rolls please." Sonya tossed the roll to Elise. "Go fix it."

Elise gritted her teeth and refilled the spindle. After double-checking the bathroom, she searched for her boss again.

She found Sonya in the kitchen in the middle of a rant. The chef stared at a warming plate, his face alarmingly red. "Fix it!" Sonya pointed a finger before turning to Elise.

"Did you clear this food?"

Elise nodded, again not knowing what was wrong.

"The food is very pedestrian looking." Sonya sniffed before fixing a steely glare on Elise. "How could you accept it?"

"Wha—" Elise started. She looked down at the food. Rosemary-charred chicken. Glazed pork chops. Twice baked potatoes. It looked okay to her.

"You should have refused to allow him to set such low standards. I'm not paying you just so I can later babysit you." Sonya spun around and waltzed out of the kitchen.

Elise glanced up at the chef. His hands trembled and he grabbed the closest thing to him—a knife— and stabbed it into the center of his cutting board. He looked at her as if daring her to say anything. Elise watched the knife's handle quiver from the thrust, and eyed the crack in the board. She swallowed and turned to follow her boss out as quickly as possible.

Chapter 5

The wedding went off without a hitch, with a very happy bride and groom dancing late into the evening at the reception. Before Elise had left to go home, Sonya had handed her an unmarked sealed envelope. As soon as Elise had walked through the door of her home, she'd thrown the envelope, unopened, onto her kitchen counter. The only thing on her mind at the time was to immediately remove the torture devices — aka high heels — and walk around on the cool floor, barefoot.

This morning, she spotted the envelope as she poured herself a mug of coffee. After first adding a bit of cream and sugar, she took the steaming mug and the letter to her favorite morning spot, her cozy window seat.

It was seven am, and the sun was just able to peep over the roof of the house across the street, raising a thin coat of fog as it heated the shingles. Elise leaned back against the pillows and tucked her feet under her blue and green afghan — one she'd made while home sick a few years ago. She took a sip of her coffee and savored the sweet roasted taste on her tongue.

Max jumped up next to her and butted her knee a few times, his tail lashing. Elise scratched his ears and smiled at his contented eyes. He closed them completely as his purr rolled through his chest. She leaned to kiss his hard head. "You're my baby, aren't you?" she whispered.

Smiling, she lifted the envelope and quickly opened it. Inside was a thin note wrapped around her first paycheck. The note was simple, stating in clear print, **No time off. See you tomorrow at noon. One more wedding to go.**

She looked at amount of the paycheck and grimaced. Seriously? Was it even worth it? These last few days had been brutal...let alone having to daily face Sonya's wrath. Sighing, she slid the note back into the envelope. She settled back against the cushions to look out the window with the mug cupped in her hand, relishing the heat that traveled into her fingers.

Better drink it up. Only a few hours until it starts all over again.

Out of the blue, a feeling of heaviness descended on her. It was frustrating because after all, her life was good. She loved her town, loved her friends. Her cat was the best ever.

But in the midst of everything going on, she wondered what her own legacy would be.

Maybe I'm here just to meet one person. To impact one person's life, even a stranger.

Max butted her leg again and pulled her from her introspection. She took another sip of her coffee. *Girl, maybe you need to get out there and run these feelings off.*

Deciding that was the case, she went in search of her tennis shoes. That took a bit, since she hadn't jogged in over two weeks, but finally they were located under the couch. She sat on the floor and laced them up, relishing the tight grip on her foot. That grip reminded her that somewhere inside of her was a strength. After all, she'd competed in a half-marathon, and that was nothing to sneeze at; especially considering before that training, she'd never exercised a day in her life.

That strength wasn't something she tapped into often, but it was there when she needed it. A spark.

As she thought about it, she realized the spark had been there other times in her life. *Like the night I found out Mark cheated on me. I'd felt so alone.* She remembered how she'd reacted, half-screaming, half praying, filled with fear, rejection. Shame that everyone else had known. Out of nowhere, a warmth had come over her and somehow, deep inside her heart, she'd no longer felt alone.

Max joined her and Elise scratched his head. "I guess that's the reason for the job, lil' buddy. To keep the both of us fed." The cat slit his eyes in response and purred.

Ok, shake it off. Can't stay in this deep spot or it'll suck me down. So in the meantime…

…I'm going to run.

She stood up and stretched, feeling her thigh muscles burn as she slid into a lunge. Then, after a quick search for her keys — *in what parallel universe do I live that these suckers keep disappearing from where I know I left them!* — she locked the front door. A quick flip on her phone pulled up her play list, then she pushed in her ear buds and started to run.

Her first half mile was slow and easy, feet pounding on the sidewalk. She ignored the barking dogs and the cars that whizzed by. Her steps ate up block after block as she steadily increased her speed. But about half-way through her playlist, her lungs burned and her legs screamed for her to slow down. *Give up. You can't do it.*

She clenched her jaw and pushed on farther.

My biggest obstacle is always myself. I wonder if other people have that struggle with themselves, or if it's just me.

After another twenty minutes she found herself jogging downtown. She passed the bridal shop where she'd watched the jewelry store get burglarized. It made her shiver, which felt weird since she was jogging. All those painters. The people in the diner next door watching from their tables with mouths open wide.

The alley next to Grandstone Jewels caught her attention.

Quickly, she looked both ways and darted across the road.

Elise slowed to a walk in front of Kelli's Diner with her hands resting on her hips, trying to catch her breath. A couple customers who sat in booths inside the restaurant looked at her curiously through the windows and she smiled.

Just a few more steps led her to the edge of the building where the alleyway between the restaurant and jewelry store began.

What had attracted her here? An alleyway was nothing to run down blindly, especially after some of the characters Elise had seen before roaming the town. But in broad daylight, she felt confident that she was safe enough to at least take a peek. So far, her hunches had never led her astray.

So far....

Light showed at the end of the alley where it connected to the street behind the buildings. Everything looked clear so Elise headed down.

The alley smelled of cat pee and garbage. She made it to the end and looked behind the buildings to Grandstone Jewels. The jewelry store's back entrance was locked with a steel door. Other than a few cars parked along the side of the street, everything looked empty.

Nothing to see here. I'd say that's a zero for the hunch. She turned and headed back.

Something sparkled about halfway up the alley, buried amidst beer bottles, wet newspapers, and plastic bags. Elise picked her way toward it trying to avoid the darker, more decomposed and undefinable trash. It sparkled brighter, making her heart speed with excitement.

She leaned over to scoop it up, first needing to give it a shake to remove a dangling piece of yarn.

Something clattered behind her and made Elise jump. She spun around and watched the can roll to a stop. She shivered. Rats, maybe?

Glancing back at the object, she turned it over in her hand. It was the heel from a stiletto, covered in green rhinestones, and ending with a black rubber cap. The top had four holes where it had snapped off the shoe.

Interesting. She tucked it into her hoody pocket and continued on her way back out to the street.

At the corner, she began jogging again. The shoe heel bumped against her hip. What woman, dressed to the hilt, would be down in an alley like that? Or had some poor woman been dragged there?

Reaching for her phone, she thumbed the music louder to wipe out the vision.

Wait, are there scrape marks on it? Something consistent with a violent act? She reached into her pocket and felt the heel. It seemed solid. Even the crystals felt intact, although she'd have to check it closer when she got to Lavina's house.

Because, really, where else could she go for an expert opinion on the heel?

Maybe someone had a clumsy misstep. That was the only way she could imagine this happening. Just someone running and having an accidental turn of the ankle.

But who would be running down an alleyway?

How long had the heel been there? Even though it had been in the garbage, it was remarkably clean. Was it something the police missed, or had it been left since then? Elise didn't often wear heels anymore, but even she knew this wasn't the color of heel that someone would normally wear at night. Black or nude was what was in, not this green iridescent gem.

Is there a club close by? She shook her head. She couldn't think of one. Just Kelli's Diner, hardly the place you'd wear a heel like that.

Elise turned down the next street, Adderson Way. Five houses down was Lavina's gorgeous house with its filigree-edged, wrapped porch. She stopped at the top of the driveway, hands entwined at the back of her neck and her chest heaving for breath.

Lavina's Camaro was missing.

Are you serious? Is she with Mr. G? She pulled out her phone and quickly texted.

Vi! Where are you?

The response was immediate, like she expected. Lavina never let her down.

At the shop. Why?

Elise rolled her eyes. Of course. Lavina did actually work from time to time, but always without rhyme or reason. She came and went as she pleased. Still, the deli was Lavina's baby.

Elise texted back—**I'll be right there. I've got something to show you.**

It'd better be an engagement ring.

Elise nearly choked. *Is she crazy?*

No! It's something I found behind Kelli's Diner.

You better not have stumbled into another mystery. So help me….

Elise grinned as she texted back. **Relax, Vi. I found it while jogging. How much trouble could I get into?**

Chapter 6

Sweet Sandwiches Deli was just as packed as ever, with the red-headed proprietor slicing ham behind the counter, looking contrary to her glamorous makeup and frilly apron. The scent of pepperoni and creamy cheese filled the air.

"Hi, darlin'," Lavina called. Several customers turned around to see who she was greeting. "Go on to the back room. I'll be there in just a second."

Instead of leaving, Elise watched from the end of the counter. It always tickled her to see Lavina working. She plopped the meat on the scale before wrapping it up in a plastic bag. "You want some cheese with that? I have a fresh loaf of Havarti that came in yesterday. Maybe half-a-pound? It'll melt in your mouth, it's so smooth and buttery." Lavina dragged out the last word and the man's eyebrows jumped. He nodded as the corner of his lip turned up.

Lavina briskly walked to the cooler and retrieved the half-wheel of white cheese. With a measured eye, she slid a pearl-handled knife through it and then weighed it. "Sliced?" she asked him, her green eyes flashing.

The poor guy was no match for Lavina, and eventually left the deli with another variety of cheese, two containers of Mediterranean olives, and a pound of her best roast beef.

"You've got this, Tom?" Lavina checked with her employee. At his nod, she removed her apron and gestured Elise toward the back room. "All right, show me what you've got," she said as she led the way.

Elise followed, her stomach rumbling as she left the lunch meat.

"You hungry?" Lavina asked, smiling at the noise.

"I didn't think so, but every time I come in here I'm suddenly starving."

"Tom! Bring back some Italian salami and a few slices of the basil cheese!" Lavina called to the front before leading the way to the break room.

Elise settled down into a chair at the formica table while Lavina fiddled with the single-serve coffee machine. She filled two mugs and carried them over.

"Alright," Lavina sighed, the kind that expressed the rush of relief of finally being off her feet. "Show me what you have."

Elise fiddled the heel out of her pocket and placed it on the table. She grabbed her mug and took a sip, peeping at her friend from over the top.

Lavina picked it up and examined the heel. Setting it down, she sent it spinning with one long manicured nail.

"Dolce & Gabbana," she announced with a raised eyebrow. Tom showed up with a plate of deli food, which he set on the table before hurrying out.

Elise picked up a slice of salami and layered it with a slice of cheese. She stuffed it in her mouth, hoping Lavina had more to add.

Instead of talking, Lavina leaned back in her chair with her arms crossed. "Don't look at me like butter wouldn't melt in your mouth. Where'd you find this, and what kind of trouble are you in?"

Elise swallowed and felt a zing of unfairness. "What? Why would you think this? Everything is fine."

"Really? Well, you come waltzing in here with a snapped off heel of a seven hundred dollar shoe. And you found it where?"

Elise hesitated just a second before confessing, "In the alley way."

"Where?"

"Behind the jewelry store."

"Elise! You promised you wouldn't go to creepy places alone anymore!"

"Seriously, I didn't think it was all that creepy. I saw it sparkling and just wanted to check it out."

"The same thing could have happened to you that happened to this poor girl!"

"You think something violent happened, too?" Elise reached for another piece of cheese. "The only thing is, there isn't any damage to the heel. I'd expect there to be marks if she'd been dragged. Or gouges if she kicked at the ground."

Lavina frowned and turned the sparkling heel over. "You're right. It just looks like it snapped off as if she tripped." She slid it across the table back to Elise. "So, why does this have your curiosity?"

"I thought it looked expensive and you just confirmed it. Why would she be behind the bank in the alleyway? I can't even think of a reason."

"Maybe you should show Brad just in case there's a missing person's report."

Elise nodded and made herself another salami cheese stack. "Or it could even be a clue to the Craigslist Bandits. Maybe some snazzily-dressed lady is the one doing all these hold ups."

"Draped in the jewels she steals," Lavina joked back.

Elise felt a buzz in her pocket and, shoving the stack of cheese into her mouth, she reached for the vibrating phone. Her brow wrinkled. *Who is that text from?* "Um," she tried to remember what they were just talking about. "I'm planning on showing him tonight. Anyway, I have to get back to work." She shoved the phone back in her pocket.

"Oh, my good heavens! How ancient is that phone? It still uses buttons, for crying out loud. You need to replace it right away."

"Don't remind me, Vi. It's a bummer that my iPhone met its demise in the toilet, but I can't afford a new one right now. So, I'm embracing the buttons."

"You are just to easy-going." Lavina shook her head as she then appraised Elise's attire. "And, when are we going to go on that shopping trip? Because you desperately need it. Poor Brad doesn't realize you may own something besides yoga pants and t-shirts."

Elise winked. "Oh, he knows."

A smile crept across Lavina's face. "That's what I'm talking about. Get it, girl. So how is the new job going?"

"Makes dog walking look like a dream job."

"Well, aren't you all butterflies and ice-cream this morning." Lavina responded drolly.

"It's the way I'm coping with the new boss. Coffee and sarcasm."

Lavina studied her carefully. "Oh, darlin'. You really are hating on this job, aren't you?"

Elise sighed and set the mug down. She spun it in a slow circle as she shrugged. "It's not that I hate the job. I actually loved meeting Catalina, and I can see a cool potential to help brides, calm them down, and have a hand in making one of the most important days of their lives happen the way they expect. It's just that Sonya is so darn unpleasant. I can't figure out what makes her tick yet."

Lavina nodded and picked up a piece of salami. "It's perfectionism. Makes her business amazing, but probably makes her a bear to work with. I've heard I have a touch myself."

Elise snorted. "A touch?"

A lifted eyebrow warned Elise that Lavina wasn't playing. She squashed her smile and continued. "Sonya does have it together. Her mind works a million miles a minute and she's able to pull all these details together and just make things happen. It probably helps that she's scary," Elise laughed. "So people darn well jump when she says jump."

"But," Lavina lifted a finger. "What about friends? Does she have any friends?"

"Hard to imagine, unless she just knows them on the phone. Then again, she's not someone who's warm and cuddly, so I haven't asked her to tea myself."

Lavina rolled her eyes at Elise. "I can't tell if you're being facetious or serious. Honestly, Elise. Maybe you should bring her some of my macarons," she tipped her head to indicate the front of the store, "and see if a little food helps warm her heart."

Elise smiled. "Maybe. What can it hurt?"

Her phone vibrated again and she pulled it out again. "Who the heck is this?"

"What's the matter?"

"I'm getting weird text messages. Here, hang on a second." She clicked through to open her text messages.

I'm coloring my hair and I'm thrilled!

What the heck? She scrolled to the next message.

Where are you? I might need help.

Elise bit her lip, studying the foreign number. She quickly texted back.

Who is this again?

Dots rotated in the background to show someone was typing.

"Besides," Lavina said. "Maybe you're being hard on her."

Elise was lost again. "What?"

"Your boss. Maybe you just need to get to know her better." Lavina blinked sagely.

"Well, you're feeling generous today," Elise said before glancing back at her phone. The dots still spun without a response. Sighing, she crammed it into her hoody pocket. "I'll remind you to give your next employee a chance the next time they mix up your Smoked Gouda with your Swiss."

"Har, har, har. It's just that not everyone deals with stress the way you do." Lavina's gaze flicked down to Elise's sneakers. "Running and stuff." She said the last two words with a sniff.

"I actually think Sonya deals with her stress with a tattoo addiction. But I'll consider the possibility that I'm reading her wrong. I did meet her at the most stressful point of this whole wedding thing."

"Well, you know what I always say," Lavina said, looking wise. "Trust in that gut of yours."

Elise's phone buzzed again.

Chapter 7

The deli door jingled as Elise exited, and the cold breeze lifted her hair. She zipped up the hoody and buried her nose into the collar since her body had completely cooled down since her earlier run.

Okay, I need to get home and changed and mentally prepare for Sonya. Her pocket vibrated again and she yanked out the phone with irritation. This time two texts waited.

The first one stated, **It's Catalina. Sonya gave me your number**

Her brow furrowed in frustration. *What? She's passing out my number now? So not okay with that.* She gritted her teeth together. *I need this job. I need this job.*

The second one was right to the point. **How do you know if you've left the hair coloring in too long? I think I messed up.**

A groan fell from Elise's mouth as she tucked the phone away. Not even bothering with the music list, she began to jog home. *What do I know about hair coloring? Has she not seen me? Hello, plain brown hair chucked into a ponytail.* The said ponytail swung with indignation. *I hope she's not going to ask me for help, because I seriously don't have a clue. Why on God's green earth would Sonya give her my number? Is this going to be a thing now?*

Back at home, Elise was half-way through cleaning up for work when her phone buzzed again. She grabbed it, flirting with the idea of throwing it in the garbage disposal. Picturing the grinding noise gave her a fierce grin. This time there was no doubt who the text was from.

Go meet Catalina at the Cozy Clippers ASAP

Elise's eyelids fluttered closed. What did Sonya expect her to do at the hairdresser's? She finished brushing her hair, and went on her hunt for her car keys. Max followed, hot on her heels. Finally finding them, she looked down at the orange cat. "You need a snack?"

He blinked at her.

She reached for the kitty treats and shook a few out into her hand. "Be a good boy. I'll be home soon," she cooed, setting them at his feet. He looked at them disinterested, but she knew what was up. Max was a shy eater and ignored food until he knew he wasn't being watched. At the door she took a peek and smiled as she caught Max batting one with his paw.

Cozy Clippers seemed empty and Elise found a spot to park in the front. She shut the car door with a growing knot in her stomach. *Please oh please oh…..*

She opened the salon's door and stopped cold. No amount of pleasing or ohhing was going to make this go away.

Catalina Petrovitsky sat in the beautician's chair, smiling just as happy as a clam. Unbeknownst to her, the stylist behind her held out a pair of scissors in one hand and a chunk of white cotton fuzz in the other. The look of horror on the stylist's face was evident to Elise from across the room.

Elise girded herself with a neutral mask. *Walk over with that darn glide thing. Smooth, in control. Nothing's wrong.* The hairdresser dropped the chunk of hair to the floor and slid it from Catalina's view with her foot.

"Elise!" The bride-to-be squealed as she spotted her. Elise nodded with what she hoped was a reassuring smile as she approached.

"So, what's going on here?" Elise's gaze flicked between the hairdresser and Catalina. The hairdresser's face was as pale as a sheet and she chewed on her bottom lip. "Catalina?"

"Oh, I wanted my hair to be super blonde…." It was here that Elise noticed Catalina's eyes had an extra mania to them. *Oh dear.* "I did it myself. I really thought it would be no big deal. After all, performers change their hair color all the time."

Elise's eyes watered at the sight of Catalina's orange roots. "Was peroxide involved?"

Catalina's calm facade teetered briefly as her bottom lip trembled. "My friend, Moria, said she did it that way all the time," she whispered. "and then I got distracted."

"Distracted?" Elise prompted.

"Cook called and I lost track of the time." She smiled brightly again, that peppy attitude of hers rallying. "But it's okay. Peggy here is a wizard at this kind of stuff. Right, Peggy?"

The hairdresser cleared her throat, before giving a small nod. "I'll do my best. What about a pixie cut?"

"A..." The word seemed to catch in Catalina's throat. "Pixie?"

"With the right tiara and veil, it will be so lovely," Elise rushed in. "You'll make a statement."

Peggy cast grateful eyes at Elise, thankful for the life-line. She quickly followed with, "I think I saw it on Vera Wang's runway last week. You'll really be the cutting edge."

"Talk about making memories!" Elise trilled.

"There won't be a wedding around like it." Peggy drew the comb through the hair again. She closed her eyes as it caught another rat's nest. Resignedly, she reached for her conditioner spray and dosed the knot. Little rivulets of water ran down Catalina's cheek, who wiped them with the back of her hand. She looked at the drop questioningly. "I didn't realize I was crying. Usually the valium takes care of that."

Elise sucked at her teeth. "It's not tears. It's the spray."

Catalina tried to nod when her head was jerked back by the comb's short jabs.

"How ya doing, honey?" Peggy asked.

"Never better," Catalina answered, her eyes wide.

Elise suppressed a smile as her imagination conjured up the most inappropriate picture of a wet cat. *Poor Catalina.*

Sighing, Peggy brought out the scissors again. Elise dragged over a stool closer to Catalina and took out her itinerary. "So, let's go over this together." She propped the binder up on her knees so Catalina could see.

Catalina squinted to read. "Does that say clowns?"

Elise turned the list around abruptly. *Clowns?* "No, I think what you're looking at is gowns. As in, a reception gown you can change into after the wedding."

Catalina's eyes grew dreamy. "I like clowns. I want fifty! All with green noses that match my wedding flowers. In fact, I'll have my entire wedding party wearing their circus garb." She closed her eyes and punctuated with her finger held in the air, "I bet I can get Argo, the sword swallower, to officiate."

Dear heavens. How strong is that stuff she's on? "Oh, wow. I'm not sure about that. Catalina? A circus wedding?"

Catalina shifted forward to whisper, causing Peggy to lean over the back of the chair to work on her hair. "My pa loves clowns. I need my pa to be happy. You want my pa to be happy, don't you?" The bride-to-be's bottom lip trembled yet again. The poor woman was looking half clown-like herself, with her smeared mascara and bleached-white spiky hair.

"Um," Elise hurriedly ran her finger through the list on the binder as if searching for something. "I'll need to contact Sonya. I'm just the...."

"You're my advoca... adver... My companion." Catalina patted Elise's hand. "You matter. I need you. I care about you. You go stand up for me and make my dream circus wedding come true."

Sonya is going to kill me. She wanted me to just come and babysit, and here I have a bride with fried hair wanting a passel of clowns at a circus wedding.

Elise took a deep breath. "How about if you discuss this with Cook first and then get back to me? Maybe the four of us can sit and talk about it."

"Four?" Catalina's eyes struggled to focus on Elise. She closed one, making the remaining blue eye appear overly large.

"You and I, Cook and Sonya." Elise counted on her fingers.

Still squinting, Catalina looked hard at the fingers before flopping back in the seat. Peggy withdrew the scissors just in the nick of time, preventing Catalina from impaling herself. The beautician's cheeks puffed out with exasperation as she bit back whatever exclamation had come to her mind.

"I just need you," Catalina continued. She crossed her pink sweatpants-clad legs. "Just you." Using a shooing motion, she continued. "Go. Make it happen."

Elise looked at the ground feeling defeated. She glanced at Peggy who shrugged and dropped another clump of hair into the trash. Her face tightened into the fakest smile she'd ever made as she stood and gathered the binder and purse. "All right, Catalina. I'll see what I can do."

"Everyone with a nose! Like my sash!" Catalina exclaimed, rushing up from the chair like a rocket. She wobbled like a caricature of a KO'd prized fighter. "Whoooa," she murmured, before collapsing back into the seat. "Somebody's got to do something about these floors."

Catalina patted her brittle hair and Peggy cringed.

Elise gave a confident wave, "You're in good hands, Catalina!" She hurried out the door wondering how in the world she was going to break this to Sonya.

Chapter 8

The sun had lifted off the morning dew and warmed up the sidewalk as Elise hurried to the Wedding Dreams Boutique. The air was still crisp but held the scent of a fresh rain and cherry blossoms. She could believe spring was finally here.

The bell jingled as she opened the door. Sonya was in her office typing on the computer. Biting her cheek, Elise tapped on the door.

"Come on in. You don't have to knock. Just hang on a sec while I finish this," Sonya's fingers flew over the keyboard with noisy clacking.

Elise shoved her hands into her pockets, then pulled them out again. She spun her bracelet before crossing her arms, only to return her hands to her pockets once again.

Sonya finally looked up. A wrinkle creased between her eyebrows. Not the wrinkle Elise wanted to see. "What's wrong? Your fidgeting is driving me nuts."

"So," Elise began. The words seemed to stick in her mouth. "Uh, Sonya, I hate to say this but I think we have a problem."

Sonya's eyebrow lifted, raising another wrinkle in her forehead. "I don't have time for this. What's going on?"

"Well," Elise tried again. "I went to Cozy Clippers like you said. But it was a nightmare. Catalina was in the throes of an emergency haircut when she announced that she wanted a circus-themed wedding in honor of her father."

Sonya's mouth dropped open to reveal silver caps on her bottom molars. Her fingers picked at a piece of tape on her arm where Elise noticed a fresh tattoo covered with Saran wrap.

Elise hurried to explain, "I'm sorry. I didn't mean for that to happen. I think the idea was Valium induced."

"What am I going to do now?" Sonya's face fell in despair. "Is it not bad enough that she wants to get married in two weeks? Now I have to find a circus tent and clowns? She has to be joking."

"She definitely wasn't joking, but she might yet change her mind. Once," Elise bit her lip, "everything wears off."

Sonya wasn't listening anymore. With her hands firmly clapped over her eyes, she shook her head. "I'm gonna be the laughing stock of the town. I'll never hear the end of it." Red tinged her normally pale cheeks.

"Don't worry. Somehow, we'll figure this out. Maybe she'll change her mind by tomorrow."

Sonya reached for the phone, knocking a binder to the floor. "I need to get hold of her fiancé and let him know. There's just no way this can happen."

Elise picked up the binder, noticing it was open to the expense report. Several of the past weddings venues were listed and a few numbers caught her eye. "Wow. The Petrovitsky wedding really is worth a lot." She blushed, hoping her boss didn't think she was being nosy. "Anyway, tell him this could escalate into her wanting a petting zoo with pony rides."

"Don't even joke about it. That's terrible." Still, Sonya's mouth quirked up at the corner.

Spurred on by Sonya's slight smile, Elise rambled on. "Maybe they can have a kissing booth over the altar and instead of a wedding cake, they'll have a cotton candy machine."

Sonya made a face. It quickly changed to into stiff professionalism as Cook answered on the other end. She thumbed on the speaker and set the phone in the middle of the desk.

"Hello, Cook. I'm glad I was able to get a hold of you. I wanted to discuss the possibility of a meeting with both you and Catalina tonight?"

"Sure. What's going on?" Cook's deep voice answered.

"Well, we were informed by Catalina today of a possible wedding theme change. Elise met with her. You know how we are already under the gun with a two week deadline. Well, these new ideas are acting like the proverbial monkey wrench to our plans."

"Really? She still wants to marry me, right?" His voice was tinted with amusement.

"Oh, of course. But you're gonna think this is awesome," Elise bluffed with a wink at Sonya. "Actually, what she said is that she wants a circus-themed wedding."

Cook's laugh cut her off, making both Elise and Sonya smile in relief. Finally, he said, "That's my Catalina. Always changing things up and making life crazy."

Sonya scratched at the plastic wrap. "Isn't that the craziest thing you ever heard?"

"Well," Cook said. "I can't believe she said that. But it's really not a bad idea."

Sonya's laugh choked to a stop in her throat. "I'm not sure I understand. You must see how this would be impossible."

"I mean her dad is a carny and everything," Cook continued. "It'd be a nice tribute to her family. Besides, it has a double meaning because I actually took her to the carnival on our first date."

As she listened, Sonya's mouth pressed into two white lines. She glanced desperately at Elise.

Elise tried again, "Well, Cook, it might be kind of difficult to pull off without having it look silly. Also, another thing to consider is that a lot of people are scared of clowns. You may end up actually frightening all of your guests."

Cook laughed. "Her entire family are carnies. And it might do my side some good to have a few scares. I'm actually liking this idea more and more."

The two women fell quiet, with only the ticking of the clock breaking the silence. Sonya rubbed the back of her neck. "How about if you and Catalina take the evening to think about this and we'll talk in the morning. Honestly, I'm just not sure I can pull this one off. We steer more toward fairytale weddings."

Cook cleared his throat, which sounded loud over the speaker, and his next words were patronizingly slow. "Doesn't your ad say that you make the bride's dream come true?"

Sonya winced.

"After all," Cook continued. "This is her dream, and so I guess that makes it my dream too. Money's no object. You guys need to make this happen because we only plan on getting married once."

Sonya closed her eyes, and her eyelids fluttered in stress. Elise could almost feel her boss's will shriveling in defeat.

"Okay, Cook," Sonya said. "I'll look into it. But please, think about it just a little bit more. Give me a call in the morning if you both decide this really is the direction you want to go in. Take the night to give those emotions a bit of time to subside. I did hear she had a doozy of a day with her hair."

"I'll talk to her tonight and let you know for sure tomorrow."

They said their goodbyes and Sonya hung up. Thoughtfully, she rolled the cell phone in her hand before glancing at Elise. "I'm not sure what we've gotten ourselves into. This has the potential to put me out of business."

Elise shook her head adamantly. "No! Don't even think that way. We'll totally figure this out and rock this circus wedding. Don't worry about it." She smacked the table. "In fact, it's gonna be such a rocking wedding that we'll be famous for it and people will come from all around just so we can put on their circus weddings."

Sonya sighed. "When I said I was gonna make a bride's dream come true I wasn't expecting novelty weddings."

"Well, some people are into novelty weddings. It's becoming all the rage. I've heard of medieval weddings and gamer weddings. Trust me, this will be great." Then Elise laughed. "At least she's not asking for a unicorn."

Sonya pointed at her with a fierce scowl. "Don't even joke about that."

❀ ❀ ❀

The rest of the day passed in the type of frenzy that didn't accomplish anything. Sonya was busy on the phone trying to locate a government official to clear a permit for a circus tent at the local park, while Elise called wedding dress shops to find out the different types of wedding attire they offered. So far, she was three for three on having them hang up when she got to the line "And clown suits? Do you carry those?"

The two women left at six with Sonya promising she'd call Elise as soon as she heard anything.

Back at home, Max did his normal meow greeting from the top of the china buffet as Elise came in and dumped her purse and keys. The sparkling heel on the kitchen table caught Elise's attention. The day had gone so long, she'd forgotten about her morning adventure in the alley.

Max jumped down with a loud thump and sauntered over to rub his head against her ankle. Elise smiled to see the empty space where the cat treats had been from the morning and reached into the bag for a few more.

"You have a good day, ol' boy," she said, scratching his back. He ignored the treats and blinked up at her as his purr began to roll.

Hmm, no yummy dinner smells. That meant Brad wasn't there, unusual since he normally beat her home when he worked the third shift. She hurried to the freezer for some breaded chicken and dumped the box unceremoniously onto a cookie sheet. She shoved it into the oven. Then, glancing at the clock, she hurried to her room to change her shirt and brush her hair.

A few minutes later, she heard the familiar key at the door. Brad walked in dressed in his police uniform.

"Hey, sweetie," she said before snuggling into his arms. "You work late?"

"All questions will be answered after a kiss." He grabbed her and gave her a scratchy kiss. As they pulled away, he stroked her chin with his thumb. "Sorry about that." He pooched his lips out and gently kissed her chin. It made her laugh and she pushed away. "Tell me why you're late."

"I got a tip on a suspect in the Grandstone Jewelry store robbery. And you'll never guess who."

Chapter 9

Brad bounced up and down on his toes with a big grin. Elise noticed the sparkle in Brad's eye that matched his hyperness. He always acted this way when things started to come together in his investigations.

"Well? Don't keep me in suspense? Who?" Elise asked.

"Emily Rose, waitress extraordinaire. Winner of the last three months' employee of the month at Kelli's Diner."

"You're kidding me. The restaurant right next to the jewelry store?"

"Yep." His grin grew even bigger, if that was possible. "Get this, she hasn't been back since the day of the robbery. Disappeared at the same time. And, get this, she'd been telling her co-workers that she was going leave it all to escape to a new life."

"Whoa...."

"Yep." Brad sniffed the air. "What's that I'm smelling? I'm starving!"

"Oh!" Elise's hand flew to her mouth. She ran into the kitchen and yanked open the oven door to reveal very crispy-looking chicken. Biting her bottom lip, she flashed him a guilty grin. "Golden black. I'm sure it's still delicious."

He had followed her and now looked over her shoulder at the chicken pieces. "Doesn't look too bad at all." Swinging around, he opened the fridge. "We still have the salad from last night?"

He spotted the bowl before she had a chance to respond, and pulled it out along with the ranch dressing. Elise set the cookie sheet on the top of the stove with a clatter and reached for the plates. Soon, they were dished up, with Max sitting in the middle of the kitchen floor slowly blinking at them.

Brad tossed a piece of the burnt chicken skin toward the cat. Max didn't even turn his head to look.

"So, tomorrow I'm headed to the diner to do some interviewing. Wanna come?" He crunched on a piece of chicken and hurriedly took a drink of water.

"Is that a date?" she asked, teasing him with her toe dragging along his leg.

He grinned and reached for her foot. "Of course it's a date. You free for lunch?"

"I think I can get away for a quick lunch. But things are pretty crazy at work." Quickly, she filled him in on Catalina's wedding plans.

"Well, you might be able to get a tent from the actual circus. It's over at the next town." Brad pushed up his shirt sleeves and leaned back with a satisfied sigh.

Elise's mouth dropped open. "I forgot about that! Some guy was telling me about it the other day." She made a face and grabbed his arm. "I'm so dense. I bet that's Catalina's family. She'd mentioned that her family was in town."

"Mmm. Might explain her wedding theme."

"Yeah. She said she wanted to honor her sick dad." Elise glanced over at the counter. "Hey, that reminds me that I had something to show you." She got up and retrieved the sparkling, green heel from where it'd been hidden from sight under a discarded kitchen towel. "Look what I found." She handed it over to him.

Brad's forehead wrinkled as he spun the heel in his hand. He set it on the table and looked at her. No words, just gave her that look.

"What?" she asked, feeling slightly nervous.

"You getting into trouble again?"

"Pish," she said, waving a hand as though he were ridiculous. "Please. I found it while jogging."

"Jogging where?"

She licked her lips before shrugging casually. "Behind the jewelry store."

He closed his eyes and groaned. "No. Not again."

"I swear it was just a fluke. I'm not getting involved." She reached for his hand and squeezed it.

"I'm starting to second guess that date of ours. You don't need any more intrigue."

"Stop! It was just sitting there, so I went and grabbed it."

"Grabbed it, huh? No thought that it might be a crime scene, fingerprints…."

She blanched and covered her mouth. "Oh, crap. I guess I did do it again. I'm sorry."

Brad sighed and studied the heel again. "Well, it's highly unlikely it would hold a finger print, anyway."

"I love you."

He laughed. "What did you say?"

Winking at him, she crawled into his lap and looped her arms around his neck. "You heard me."

Max watched them for a moment before deciding there wouldn't be any more chicken. He flounced out of the room, tail in the air.

❋❋❋

The next morning, 7:05 a.m. found Elise running breathlessly into the Wedding Dreams Boutique. She was furious with herself. This was no time to be late.

"Good morning. Catalina just called," Sonya flashed her a brittle smile "To let me know that her uncle will be joining us this morning." The blonde woman grabbed her paperwork and tapped it into an organized pile. "Apparently, they want to discuss the circus theme."

"Oh, she's coming with reinforcements, huh?" Elise pulled off her sweater and hung it on the back of her chair.

"You're going to take her to go look for dresses later this afternoon. But first, I've set up a cake tasting appointment for them after the meeting."

"Today? Without Cook?"

"I guess he's busy." Sonya tapped her chin thoughtfully. "You've got a lot on your hands. I'm not sure you can find a dress to match her."

"What do you mean? White matches everything."

"With that spray tan? She's so orange." Sonya wrinkled her nose. "You put her in a white dress and she'll look like she'd emptied a Cheetos bag on herself before the ceremony is over."

"Oh that's terrible."

Sonya looked in the mirror and smoothed back the gelled sides of her short hair, smiling with admiration at the blonde wave on top swooping back. "But, what am I thinking? With this circus theme, I'm fully expecting a purple gown. With rows of ribbon."

"That's so mean."

"Bedazzled," Sonya shot back. She raised her eyebrow as if daring Elise to respond.

"It's going to be okay. I'll figure this out." Elise tried to be reassuring, although not too sure of her abilities herself.

Just then, the bell dinged over the shop's entrance. Elise leaned to peek out the office door. Catalina smiled when she caught sight of her and tugged on the arm of the short man accompanying her.

The man was built like a barrel, a round chest encased in a blue jacket buttoned smartly. His face was covered in a full brown beard, which he stroked, and his lips curled up in a smile. He didn't spare a glance at the fancy decor, instead strutted in as if he owned the place.

"Uncle Rozzo, right this way. Here they are!" Catalina squealed. The man followed her with a big grin. She ran up to Elise and gave her a hug.

"Good morning," Elise murmured, smiling at Catalina. "I love your hair."

"Thank you!" The short woman tucked a short, stray curl around her ear. "I feel positively Tinkerbelle-ish."

Elise caught Sonya's big eyes at the description. She could only imagine that her boss was picturing a PeterPan/Circus chimera-type wedding. She bit back a grin. "The haircut looks great on you. Hey, it just occurred to me last night, is that your family's circus in the other town?" Her gaze swiveled from Catalina to her Uncle Rozzo.

It was Catalina who nodded. "Yes! Petrovitsky Family Circus! It's positively amazing that they're all going to be able to come to the wedding."

Sonya's mouth dropped open. "Well, that gets us out of a heap of trouble. Maybe you could get married down there?"

Catalina shook her head. "No, absolutely not. I want an outdoor wedding. Preferably at a park."

Sonya blew out a heavy sigh. "Okay." She typed on her keyboard and turned the computer monitor towards Catalina. "Here are three places I've found so far that might be available. But we have to jump quick."

Catalina leaned in to see and squealed again. "Those are absolutely fabulous! I love them all! But especially here." She tapped the screen, pointing to Angel Lake.

Sonya frowned. "Okay, I'll try for that first. But I think this one here would be more practical." She gestured to another park in a neighboring town.

"Get the first one. That's the one I want," Catalina said firmly. "It's absolutely divine."

Although it was the merest flicker of the eyebrow, it was apparent to Elise that Sonya was near her breaking point. Elise cleared her throat and addressed her boss. "Didn't you say we have a cake tasting scheduled?"

Sonya hummed a response before pushing a paper with the address across the desk. "Yes, here is the address."

"Oh, good! I know exactly what kind of cake I want. I've wanted it since I turned thirteen." Catalina said, eyes sparkling.

"Do tell," Sonya said, drolly.

"An ice cream cake!"

Sonya winced as though she had a sudden migraine. Rubbing her temple, she cleared her throat and continued. "Be sure to ask them. And, I also have a bridal shop appointment for you to try on dresses.

Think simple because there won't be a lot of time to get it fitted. Have you thought about what you want your bridesmaids to wear?"

"Yes, I think we've got that covered," Catalina nodded enthusiastically. Elise smiled. She really did look pixie-like.

Elise touched Uncle's Rozzo's arm to get his attention. "Are you going to join us for the cake testing?"

Uncle Rozzo's muscles flexed as he drew his arm away. Elise could feel how, despite his short stature, he really was quite strong. "Cake tasting, you say? I should be watching my diet, but I guess I'm game."

Catalina giggled. "Oh, Uncle. When have you ever turned down free food?"

"As long as the meal isn't being served in jail, I guess I'm always up for a bite," he countered back, smiling so hard his wrinkles nearly hid his eyes.

Chapter 10

Uncle Rozzo held the boutique's door open for the two women as they exited. He followed behind, giving a nonsensical whistle between his teeth.

"You don't mind riding in my Pinto, do you? It's pretty small. I think it's all cleaned out, but that doesn't help a lot," Elise asked. *Lovely. When was the last time I cleaned it?* She gave them a nervous grin and started rummaging in her purse for the keys.

"Oh, sugar. Us carnies aren't afraid of small spaces." Catalina giggled. "Haven't you seen the clown cars?"

Elise paused, keys in hand. "Are those a real thing?"

Catalina laughed even harder.

"Oh, you're teasing me." Elise rolled her eyes and led them to the car.

❀ ❀ ❀

Cake testing was a success despite Catalina's new demands. Elise was rather surprised at the baker's confident attitude as he took the request. Almost blasé, as if the bakery were asked for ice-cream cakes all the time. Elise did insist that they try the samples already laid out before them—which were delicious. In the end, Catalina still remained adamant on her final choice. The cake was ordered with the chef mentioning that the final decorating always took place on site.

Elise glanced at her watch and herded them all back to her car. "I'm supposed to meet someone at Kelli's Diner right now. Would you both like to join me for lunch?" she asked.

"Honestly, I couldn't eat another bite." Catalina said, patting her stomach.

"Kelli's Diner?" Uncle Rozzo leaned forward between the seats to hear better, his bushy eyebrows furrowed questioningly.

"Yeah. It's across the street from the bridal boutique."

"I know where it is." He sat back with his arms crossed.

Elise glanced at him in her rearview mirror. His chipper attitude seemed to have ebbed away as he frowned out the window.

They arrived at the diner a few minutes later, with Elise parking outside Wedding Dreams. Elise peeked in the boutique window as they walked past, but didn't see Sonya.

The diner was busy with the lunch crowd. Uncle Rozzo stood to the side to take it all in before finally smiling at Catalina.

"Well, little girl," he kissed his niece on the head. "Thanks for letting this old man tag along today. I'm off to make a dollar. You coming by later?"

"Of course, Uncle Rozzo. I'll be there by seven."

His eyes glinted under bushy eyebrows as he smiled with apparent affection. "It's just not going to be the same without you, little Cat."

She giggled. "You know that I haven't done the trapeze in years."

"Maybe tonight, though, eh?" he asked. He laughed as she shook her head. "No? Well, soon you'll be having kids and we'll be training those 'un's right." He patted her shoulder and turned his attention to Elise. "You should come visit, too. It's not likely we'll be back in these parts for quite some time. I can give you the premier tour."

"Oh," Elise was caught off guard. "You don't have to do that. But, actually, I think I'd like to. It's been years since I've last been."

"What circus have you been to?" His eyes squinted skeptically.

"The Brandle Circus," she answered.

He let out a loud guffaw. "Those cheapskate imitators! You might as well have never been to a circus then. They feed their tigers swill and their patrons not much better. Come tonight to visit the Petrovitsky Family Circus. I'll have tickets waiting for you at the booth. Just ask for Uncle Rozzo." He touched the side of his nose and then pointed at her and winked cheerfully.

Elise couldn't help but chuckle. He definitely was a charmer! "Okay. Maybe this weekend, if I'm not working too hard." She nudged Catalina's arm.

He gave a wave as he left the diner. Elise watched as, coincidentally, he passed by Brad outside on the sidewalk.

Brad's eyes flickered when he saw Uncle Rozzo, and his mouth was drawn as he walked into the coffee shop. It relaxed into a grin at Elise's wave.

"Hey sweetie!" She hurried over to give him a hug. Mmm, he smelled like fresh air and cedar. "We have to eat quick because we have an appointment." She beckoned to Catalina. "This is my new friend and bride-to be, Catalina. And, this is my boyfriend, Brad."

"It's nice to meet you." Brad gave the petite blonde an easy smile.

As usual, she gushed with enthusiasm, "It's *so* nice to meet you. Any friend of Elise's is a friend of mine! And you just missed my Uncle Rozzo!"

He raised an eyebrow. "Really?"

"Yes," she giggled. "You just passed him on the street."

Brad jerked his thumb in the direction of the door. "That guy in the blue jacket is your uncle?"

Catalina nodded. Elise glanced at her watch and tried to gently herd them to the counter to order. They didn't have a lot of time.

Brad wasn't budging. "Interesting. I've seen him around before. Was that your aunt he was with the other day?"

Catalina's smile dropped off and her eyebrows knotted in confusion. "My uncle doesn't have a lady friend. He's been single since," here she looked up into the sky as though the answer might be up there. "Since I was just learning the tightrope."

Brad gave her a shrug. "Maybe that's just want he wants you to think. Contrary to popular opinion, men can be secretive too."

Catalina shook her head firmly before brushing down the ruffled flounce at the hem of her blouse. "Carnies aren't secretive." She caught the snort from Brad and amended, "Not among ourselves, we aren't.

We're all a big family, whether we're related or not. Besides," she grinned wickedly, "there's the gossip train. And trust me, if Uncle Rozzo were seeing anyone, that'd be all over the gossip train." She lifted her arm as though pulling a rope and sang out, "Toot, toot!"

Elise laughed despite herself. This girl was a trip. "You don't think there's anyway he could be seeing someone on the side?" And then to Brad, "Tell me about her."

"She had dark hair, cut to about here," he demonstrated with his hand to the base of his neck, "Short," his eyes flashed mischievously. "Cute," He laughed and raised his hands to fend off Elise's punch. "Not as cute as you, though."

"Short hair?" Catalina interrupted. She bit her lip and looked down.

"Yeah." The joking tone drained out of his voice at her reaction. "You know her?"

Catalina crossed her arms and shook her head in the negative. But her bubbly nature was squashed. As if to emphasize her contemplative thoughts, she sighed, then pulled out her phone and began to type.

Elise cleared her throat. "So, should we get something to eat?"

Brad nodded. "I'm starving."

"You guys go ahead and order. I'm not hungry anymore." Still typing, Catalina ignored them both. She spun around on her little heels and walked to the far side of the diner, staring at her phone.

"Well, thank you for that," Elise rolled her eyes at Brad. "As if it isn't hard enough to help a crazed woman find a dress that makes her feel good. I thought I was just going to have to do the normal, no that doesn't make you look fat, comments. But this..." she sighed. "This looks like it's going to be quite the catalyst for drama."

"Hmm. It doesn't look good, and it definitely sounds like there is more to the story." He leaned over to kiss her. "I trust you to skulk it out."

The manager headed over, attracted by Brad's uniform. His apron looked like he'd wiped his hands on it after fixing his greasy hair. He had tiny pig eyes and a tight grin. Reaching them, he stretched out his hand. "Hello! Name's Henry Dory. I'm sorry about this," he gestured to the busy restaurant. "My cook quit, too, and with Emily Rose gone, we've been short-staffed. Have a Craigslist ad out, but in the meantime," he shrugged.

Elise's ears perked up at the mention of Craigslist and she assessed the manager's height. The news had stated the other night that one of the Bandits was a tall male. That didn't jive with her idea of the robber being a fancy dressed lady who wore sparkling heels, but she wasn't ready to give that idea up.

On the wall behind the manager, she noticed eight or ten framed photos hanging on the wall, each with a plaque underneath. The photo closest to her held the title of *employee of winter season*, along with the name Emily Rose. Elise leaned closer to study the woman's features.

The waitress was slight with high cheekbones, but otherwise rather unremarkable. Elise could have passed her a hundred times in town and not remembered who she was.

"Can you tell me a little about her?" Brad asked.

More people came into the restaurant and waited to be seated. The noise grew with loud conversation and laughter.

"Not a lot to tell." Henry's face flushed and he glanced nervously at the growing crowd. "She was a hard worker, great attitude. Single." He licked his bottom lip at the mention of her being single and Elise shivered.

"Did she give any notification that she was leaving?"

Henry shook his head. "No, none at all. We'd closed together the night before, and she'd seemed fine."

"How was she the day she left? Did she appear nervous? Anxious?"

Again, Henry shook his head.

From the corner by the entrance came a squeak. Catalina's eyes were squeezed tight and her shoulders shook.

Elise sighed, realizing she had to forgo the rest of Brad's interview and her lunch. She patted his arm goodbye and cautiously walked over. "You okay, sweetie?"

Catalina nodded, still biting her bottom lip. Elise wondered how she had any lip left the way she chewed on it. "Come on. Let's go and make you pretty." She rested her hand on Catalina's arm. "Take a deep breath. We're going to have fun."

Catalina gave a shaky, pink-bubblegum lipgloss smile and tucked her cell phone back in her bra. She nodded. "You're right. I'm ready." She entwined her arm though Elise's. "Where are we going?"

✳✳✳

The two women left the shop and walked over to Elise's yellow car. Catalina dropped into the front passenger seat with a sigh.

Elise settled into the driver's seat and glanced over at the other woman. "So," she started hesitantly, "I don't want to pry, but Brad's news seemed to kind of take you off guard."

Catalina looked out the window and chewed on her thumbnail.

"I just wanted to say, I'm here if you want to talk. Or if you want to forget everything and just have fun, I'm totally down for that, too."

Catalina retrieved her phone and checked her messages. Wrinkling her nose, she shoved it back. "It's nothing. I'm sure she's just some lady he ran into. Sometimes things can just appear other than what they really are."

At the wedding dress shop, Elise swerved the car into the last parking spot with the finesse of threading a needle. What made the parking tight was a white van parked on the line, its side advertising 'Carson's Painting—We paint it all' with a cartoon man covered in blue paint.

Hogging the space on the other side of the Pinto was a black Lexus, quite an unusual sight around these parts of Angel Lake.

She'd tried to angle her car so that Catalina had enough room to climb out. It was a tight squeeze for Elise herself, and she found herself sucking in her gut to make it through. "You okay?" Elise called over the top of her car to Catalina.

"I'm just fine, ducky," Catalina called back, after shimmying down the side of the car. The two women brushed themselves off and Catalina readjusted her shirt's flounce. Together, they headed across the parking lot to the strip mall, where BRIDE'S BEST held the most prominent place on the large sign.

"So, you think they'll have something for me?" Catalina's forehead creased with worry and her dark eyelashes fluttered.

"Of course. That's why I brought you here."

"I need something big. Big. Big."

"We'll find it here."

Chapter 11

They walked into the dress shop and were instantly descended upon by two saleswomen clad in identical, tight pink dresses. At their side was a dog —a very large poodle whose pink fur was shaved to full pom-pom glory. The dog's nails clicked on the marble floor as she meandered over to check out the newcomers. Elise checked. Nails painted blue.

"Catalina?" one of the women asked. Her black hair was pulled tight into a smooth chignon at the base of her neck.

Catalina giggled as usual, before squealing out effusively, "I'm *so* delighted to be here!" She looked around the room. "It's just *absolutely* lovely."

The other saleswoman stepped in then, a blonde with a similar chignon. "I'm Allison and this is Simone. And this darling here," her hand rested on the poodle's head. "Is Cupcake! We're going to make you look so beautiful!"

"Oh hush, now." Simone sidled up, her glossed lips in a pink pout. "This sweet, young thing is already beautiful." She flashed a hundred-watt smile. "What we're going to do is accentuate that beauty."

"Make that groom of yours go ga-ga," Allison intoned with a wink.

Catalina twirled a nub of a curl around her finger before shivering with excitement. Whatever had happened between the text message and the news about her uncle seemed long forgotten.

The two women ushered her between pale peach curtains to what could only be described as a dressing room decadent enough for a Queen. White silk damask covered a round couch while beveled floor-to-ceiling mirrors provided the staging area. There was even a white, carpeted, two-step platform for the bride-to-be to stand upon and admire the long train behind her.

"Now, what are you thinking?" asked Simone as she quickly sized up Catalina with a gaze. Her eyes paused at her waist, hips, and chest as if measuring.

"Yes. Tell us about your dream dress. Mermaid? Formal? Long train?" the other consultant chipped in. "Where is the wedding being held? Is it important for your arms to be covered? What type of wedding are you having?"

Sonya's words echoed in Elise's head and all she could imagine was a Gypsy wedding dress. Would Catalina ask for pom-poms? Diamond dazzles?

Ruffles galore? She held her breath and waited for Catalina's answer.

The bride-to-be smiled. "I'd like something that's a little off the shoulder, and not too fitted," she patted her stomach area. "Here." Her cheeks turned slightly pink.

Both sales associates zeroed in on her stomach. Simone raised an eyebrow. "So you're saying...."

"I believe we'll need to delay the fitting of the dress until the last possible moment," Allison winked.

Catalina giggled and hid her face behind her hand shyly. Her eyes sparkled as she caught Elise's surprised face. "It's true. Due at the beginning of summer. My own little trapeze artist."

Her comment triggered Elise's memory. "Your uncle knows?"

With a nod, Catalina answered, "I told you. There aren't any secrets in the Carny world."

"Well, you aren't the first to come in with that beautiful glow." Simone clasped her hands together.

"We know just what to do. You'll be the most gorgeous bride ever!" Allison agreed.

"First, do you have a bathroom?" Catalina asked. Elise noticed she was fidgeting a bit from foot to foot.

"Of course! Right this way," Simone answered with a gentle nod and beckoned her to follow her.

While Simone ushered the pregnant woman to the restroom, Allison turned her attention to Elise. With bright eyes, she asked, "Can I get you some coffee?"

Elise shook her head. No, after all that sugar earlier, what she needed was a sandwich, and STAT. The consultant must have read her mind. "How about a dish of mixed nuts?" she asked with a tip of her blonde head.

"That would be incredible," Elise's stomach growled and she laughed, embarrassed.

Allison gave an amused smile. "Coming right up." She sauntered from the dressing room.

On her way out, Elise caught Allison making a pucker face and refreshing her lipstick in front of the mirror. The consultant smiled at her reflection and checked her teeth, before disappearing into another room, presumably for the snacks.

Elise spun slowly around to take the space in. There was the wall that was lined with mirrors, while the other wall displayed veils and sparkling tiaras. Elise walked over to check out the crowns, smiling a bit. The tiaras came in all forms, from fully-formed circlets, to combs holding the jeweled headpiece.

The veils were a variety lengths and styles and hung from several rotating racks. She drew her fingers through the silky fabrics. *Gorgeous.*

On the far wall stood shelves filled with shoes, looking much like the closet of a wealthy socialite. Ninety percent were colored cream or white, but the bottom shelf held an assortment of colors.

Her breath caught in her throat. There it was. The green pair. She hurried over and retrieved one from the rack. Turning it over, she noted the designer's name stamped into the bottom. Lavina had been right.

"Aren't those lovely?" Allison said.

Elise jumped at the sound of the consultant's voice and spun around, somehow feeling guilty about the heel in her hand.

"Those are more popular than you'd imagine. You never know when you might need a shamrock slipper. They might just lead you to the end of the rainbow!" Allison laughed at her own joke.

"You sell a lot of these?"

"Oh, so many. We're one of the only ones who keeps them in stock, so we have customers travel from all over to buy them. Stage performers, charity event holders, even politicians. Why, we had the governor's wife in here just last week."

Elise turned the heel over in her hand. "It really is lovely."

Allison set the dish of nuts on the coffee table. "Is that color calling to you?"

With her toes wiggling inside her sensible ballet flats, Elise could hardly keep a straight face. "No. I'm likely to break my neck wearing these."

"Nonsense. With a few lessons, you'll be walking like a run-way model." Allison apprised Elise with her critical eye. "In fact, with the right clothes...."

"One more question." Elise butted in to head off the consultant's train of thought. "Do you keep records of the people who bought the shoes?"

"Why do you ask?"

"Well, oddly enough, I found one outside a place that had recently been robbed. I was wondering if she'd seen something."

Allison raised her nose in the air. "In order to give something like that out we'd need a court order. Some things are just private, and people trust us to respect their privacy."

"I'm back and ready to play dress-up!" Catalina called as Simone trailed behind her.

Allison turned her attention to Catalina, dismissing Elise. *Well, that conversation didn't go well.* She scooped up a handful of nuts when something flickered in her peripheral vision. Elise turned to see a slender figure standing outside the boutique's window.

It was the tiny shape of a teenage girl, whose hands were cupped to see inside. She caught Elise's stare and shivered, before drawing back and hurrying away.

Chapter 12

T minus 6 on the count-down to Catalina and Cook's wedding day. Elise padded in her wooly socks and t-shirt into the kitchen. Sonya had texted and said she didn't need to come in until eleven, since Catalina would be at a fitting for her wedding dress all morning. Having the time to sit and slowly drink her coffee felt like such a luxury.

Max followed after her, his orange tail swishing. "Are you hungry, buddy?" she asked, already knowing the answer. Max was always hungry, as his hanging belly flap attested. "What's the vet going to say the next time he sees you? He's going to say, kitty diet, that's what." Max rubbed his cheek up against her leg. "Oh fine, one treat." She retrieved a treat from the bag and set it on the floor. Then she set about making her own breakfast. "Eggs this morning I think. With lots of salsa. So I can have an excuse to eat bacon."

She arranged the bacon on a cookie sheet and slid it into the oven. She'd let that bake a few minutes before starting the egg.

Elise grabbed her mug of coffee and carried it over to her happy place, her window seat framed from the outside by the cherry tree. The cushions were soft as she climbed up on it, reaching to pull her crocheted afghan up over her legs. Leaning back, she looked out at the beautiful day.

A white truck pulled up next to the neighbor across the street. Elise watched it park, her brow wrinkling thoughtfully. Looked like the painter's truck she'd seen yesterday, but no sign. And when had she seen another one? The memory flickered at the edge of her mind but she couldn't grasp it.

The driver climbed out garbed in white coveralls. He slammed the door and walked back behind the van to unlatch the louver door. After pushing it open back on its tracks, he yanked down a ramp.

As the ramp grated against the ground, the passenger climbed out of his side of the truck. He too was wearing white coveralls with a baseball cap pulled low over his forehead. He carried a clipboard and the two men briefly consulted together behind the van. The passenger chucked the clipboard into the back and the two of them headed up the walk to the front door.

So it's a moving truck? I didn't even see a for sale sign. Elise couldn't help the tinge of surprise. The neighbor woman was in her late fifties and worked at the local water company. Though it wasn't often they ran into each other, the neighbor always had a smile and a wave whenever she spotted Elise. They'd even exchanged Christmas cookies last year.

I wonder who's moving in?

Max jumped on the couch and head butted under Elise's arm for more attention. She scratched his ears and throat, and he let out a rusty meow in contentment.

"Hey buddy. Whatcha think, huh? Did you know she was moving?"

Max rubbed his head across her lips and she giggled as she kissed him. He flopped down on the window seat as his paws worked to knead the bit of blanket that had fallen from her leg. Elise stroked his side and his purr grew louder. She looked out the window again.

A green car broke her field of vision as it drove down the road. Rusty, and battered, the car looked like it had been in more than one accident in its lifetime. A pair of hands clenched the steering wheel tightly, and Elise smiled. *Better hold on to that steering wheel tight. I don't think your car can take another accident.*

As the car passed, the driver looked up her driveway.

It was the man from outside the first wedding reception. The one who'd approached her and talked about the circus.

She jerked back from the window. *Did he see me?* Heart pumping, she ducked down below the seat. Did the tree shade me enough? He seemed to have been more focused on her front door.

What's going on? Was he following me? She peeped out of the corner of the window, but the green car was long gone.

Shakily, she stood up and pulled down her blinds.

The scent of burning bacon filled the air. *Oh, crap!* Elise ran into the kitchen for the forgotten bacon. Using a towel, she whisked the tray out of the oven and onto a cutting board.

Her brow wrinkled as she looked down at the tray, not really seeing it. Her mind was a million miles away as she used the towel to fan the bacon off.

Do I call Brad? What do I say? Hey, some strange dude drove by. What if it was some bizarre coincidence? What if I didn't have a friend on the police force? I'd just have to handle it myself, right?

She unrolled a loop of paper towels onto a plate and transferred the bacon for the grease to blot off. Snagging a piece, she moved back to the front window for another peek.

He was gone. The movers across the street were all she could see.

She crunched her bacon thoughtfully as Max meowed at her feet for his share. *Time to take Uncle Rozzo up on his offer and visit the circus, apparently. Maybe Brad will come with me. If I see the green car there, I might be able to track this guy down better.*

"Why do I attract weirdos, Max?" she asked the cat who blinked adoringly up at her. *Resist. Must resist.* He gave a little "brit" from the back of his throat and stared hypnotically.

"You need to go on a diet, buddy." She looked at the bacon in her hand and sighed. "Fine, just a little piece," she murmured, breaking off one of the crispy edges. She dropped it on the floor and continued to her room to get ready. Half-way there, she detoured back into the kitchen for more bacon and her phone to text Brad. **Want to go on a Circus Date?**

Chapter 13

Elise hadn't been to the circus since she was nine years old. And since then, she'd seen enough scary movies starring clowns to waver from the child-like opinion that it was a magical place. Now circuses lay more on the creepy end of the spectrum.

While searching for a parking spot, Elise had kept an eye out for the green car. It was like looking for a needle in a haystack, though, with how the lot was jam-packed. She tried to rouse up her courage. *He doesn't know I saw him, and he has no idea I'm here.*

They passed through the entrance after picking up the tickets that Uncle Rozzo had left for them. Brad held her hand firmly, his hand feeling warm and strong.

He looked down and gave her a smile. "What are you thinking about?"

She shook her head. Giving a cop a tidbit like this was a sure way to ruin a date. And by gum, it was the first real date in a month. She wasn't ruining this one.

The circus was a bevy of colors and smells. Barnyard scents from the animals mixed weirdly with popcorn and a spice she couldn't identify. Peanut shells littered the hard-packed dirt pathway, and garbage cans stood overflowing on the corners of the tents.

Her eyebrow flickered in amusement as a fat clown skipped by leading a pony. The horse wore a sparkling halter and a pink tutu around its belly, matching the flowing tulle skirt worn by the clown.

Three small dogs came along next with another clown wearing green suspenders. This clown smiled at Elise as he passed, his painted lips large and garish. She smiled back with a feeling of uncertainty.

The clown stopped as two children reached to pet his dogs. He honked his nose in response to every question the children asked, while their parents watched with a look of indulgence.

Elise and Brad sidestepped around them. Feeling a brush on her arm, Elise looked over to see the ringmaster. She recognized him right away, with his stereotypical black coat with long tails. He carried a staff topped with a silver ball and winked at her. Then, after twirling his mustache like an old time dastardly train robber, he hurried into the main tent.

"Are you ready?" Brad asked at the tent's entrance. His eyebrows jerked with concern at the sound of a braying donkey from somewhere inside. "Am I ready?"

"Yep. This is going to be fun."

Brad handed the two pink ticket stubs to a man wearing a striped shirt stretched tight over a round body the size of a beer barrel. The man leered at Elise and switched his cigar from one side of his mouth to the other.

Once the flap closed behind them, they entered what felt like a dark cavern. Flashing spotlights highlighted the overhead trapeze swings and the large net that covered half the floor. The straw-covered the floor was also littered with barrels, giant rings and several painted ladders. The child-like excitement she'd thought she'd lost fluttered in Elise's chest as they headed for their seats.

The stands were already crowded with moms and dads and little kids shoving in each other. Hawkers climbed up and down the stands yelling, "Cotton candy! Peanuts!"

Brad kept a tight grip on Elise's hand as they squished past the people already seated, trying not to step on toes or knock over purses. Finally, they reached their seats, front and center, and settled down to look around the tent area. Having VIP tickets had its perks.

Colorful floodlights swooped around the room and splashed against floor length curtains at the back. Elise felt suitably dazzled as Brad waved down the peanut guy and ordered a bag. Suddenly, she saw someone she recognized and touched Brad's elbow.

"Look down there," she said, pointing with her pinky, "That's Catalina's Uncle Rozzo."

Brad turned to look just in time to see the man skirt behind the curtain along the back wall. "And look he's with," he grimaced.

Elise craned her neck to see who was with Uncle Rozzo. "Who?"

"The mystery lady friend I saw him with the other night."

The petite woman darted behind the curtain.

"What struck your interest the first time you saw them?" Elise asked.

"They were standing outside arguing, by that diner next to your work. He seemed a little steamed so I was keeping an eye on things."

"And?"

Brad shrugged. "They worked it out and went their separate ways."

Popcorn flew in the air from behind them and Elise felt her chair get a good whack. She turned to see two young kids fighting. Their poor mom appeared as if she hadn't slept in a decade.

Brad's muscles tensed under the flannel shirt he wore. "You know who I think that was?" The tone in his voice shot a mind bullet at her. The award picture.

"Not...."

He nodded. "You got it. Emily Rose. The missing waitress. " He kissed her cheek. "I'll be right back."

What? But the show is about to start? Instead of protesting, Elise nodded with what she hoped was an understanding look.

Standing with a broad confidence, Brad scanned the crowd around him before zeroing in on the back of the tent. He picked his way down the rows of seats to the arena floor and traveled in the last direction they'd seen Uncle Rozzo.

Elise shifted uncomfortably, keenly aware of the empty seat next to her. It seemed to radiate, "She's alone, folks! No date for her!" The kids behind her kicked her seat in a rapid succession. She gritted her teeth. She'd never been good with kids and had no idea of what to do other than turn around and yell at them. But, judging from the mom's face, that was the last thing that mom needed.

The lights lowered then, and the kids settled down. On the floor, three spotlights swooped to illuminate a single area. The ringmaster walked into the light with his hands in the air, welcoming everyone. Applause swelled and became deafening. Elise's own hands stung from clapping so hard.

The ringmaster lowered his hands and began to speak. "Ladies and Gentlemen. I proudly present to you over a hundred years of experience, tricks, and death defying acts. Hold your loved ones close and don't look away. Presenting the Petrovitsky Family Circus!"

※ ※ ※

The show was everything magical Elise had remembered from her childhood. The audience collectively gasped at the trapeze artists, cringed at the fire-breathing man, and squealed at the dogs riding on top of the elephants. Clowns somersaulted and squirted the audience with confetti-spewing plastic guns. Bears wearing paper hats rode bicycles. Women in tiny costumes twirled on ribbons that hung from the ceiling, while below, ponies with pink-painted hooves danced in rhythm.

Somewhere, between the tightrope walker and the motorcycle cage of death, Brad rejoined her. It was too noisy to hear anything, but he shook his head to let her know he didn't find anything.

When the ringmaster did his final bow, the applause was thunderous. Slowly the lights came up leading everyone to blink hard.

Elise's phone vibrated in her pocket. She fished it out to read, **You still at the circus? Cook and I are here!**

She automatically glanced around as if expecting the petite blonde and the red-headed giant to appear at her elbow. Not seeing them, she typed back, **Just leaving the main tent right now.**

The response was immediate. **Wait for us! We'll be right there.**

Tucking the phone away, Elise nudged Brad's arm. "I need to hang out here for a second. Catalina and her fiancé are coming to meet us."

He grimaced. "This has been the worst date night, ever. First my fault, and now yours."

"Sorry! What was I supposed to say?"

He grabbed her in his arms and growled into her neck. "How about, make it quick. I'm on a date with my man candy."

His breath tickled, and laughing, she drew her chin down to nudge him out. "I'll do my best." She glanced up just in time to see a thin waif of a girl with large gray eyes staring at her from over by the concession stand. The teenager seemed familiar, but

Elise couldn't place her. The girl looked up the dirt walkway and then darted away.

"Elise!" squealed Catalina enthusiastically from the direction the teen had drawn her attention to. The blonde woman swung Cook's hand as she hurried over. "I'm so glad to see you!" She gave Elise a big hug, as Brad shook Cook's hand. "So! What did you think?"

"It was amazing," Elise admitted. Which was totally true. In fact her cheeks hurt from smiling so much.

"Isn't it, though?" Catalina beamed with pride. She looped her arm through Elise's. "Let me introduce you to the guy who's going to marry us."

The little woman was strong, and Elise found herself being dragged through the funneling crowd of people back into the tent. "Argo!" Catalina yelled. "Has anyone seen Argo?"

One of the clowns pointed, and Catalina towed her in that direction. There was a man dressed in black bending over a long case. He seemed to be meticulous in the way he was arranging something.

"Ahh, Argo," Catalina chimed. "I have friends for you to meet."

The man glanced up at his name and straightened to a height rivaling Cook's, although he was considerably skinnier.

Elise recognized him as the sword swallower. "Hi. I'm Elise," she said, taking his hand. She half winced inside, waiting for his response. She couldn't help but wonder if he'd sound rusty from all those swords.

"Any friend of our little Cat's is a friend of mine," his words were low and melodious. His thumb gave a gentle rub against her hand as he smiled. Quite a charming smile, actually, accentuated by thoughtful, dark eyes.

Next to her, Brad cleared his throat. Elise blinked and dropped Argo's hand. "Brad," he said, also shaking the sword swallower's hand.

A short, stout man in a clown suit walked up to the group of them. "Howdy folks! Howdy! Howdy! Howdy!"

"Hi, Uncle Rozzo," Catalina giggled.

Uncle Rozzo stuck a rubber nose on his face and squeezed it a few times, while shimmying his chest at her, making the four colorful pompoms there dance.

"How's my girl? And what happened to your arm?"

Elise looked to see a previously unnoticed scrape on Catalina's arm. The petite blonde hid it with one hand. "You know me, always tripping on something. I fell during my wedding gown fitting yesterday."

"Ah, as graceful as ever, I see," He winked a fluffy eyebrow at her.

"Honestly, I can't take you seriously with that nose on," his niece said.

"Since when have you ever taken me seriously?" Still, he plucked off the nose and hid it away in the pocket of his striped trousers. "So, you're still going through with this marriage, eh?" He eyed Cook.

"Now, Uncle Rozzo, you know he's a good guy."

"He's not a carny though, no offense to you," this last bit was tossed up to Cook.

"Fresh blood is good, Uncle." Catalina nudged him and raised an eyebrow.

Uncle Rozzo gave her a measured look before nodding. "Yes, yes, that's right. New blood." And then with a wave as he turned to leave, Elise heard him mutter, "and new money."

Chapter 14

T minus 4 until the wedding day. Time was dwindling down. Outside Wedding Dreams, Sonya tapped the horn of her VW bus, appearing impatient through the windshield. Elise locked the boutique's door behind her, not feeling excited about the car ride ahead. She jumped in the back seat and passed the keys up front.

There'd been no question about where she would sit. They were on their way to pick up Catalina right now.

"I hate being late," Sonya's soft voice still managed to growl as she crammed the car into gear with a loud noise.

Elise didn't say anything. They weren't late. In fact, Elise had been early, knowing Sonya. But her twenty minutes early still apparently equaled late on Sonya's timetable.

They drove the two blocks to the Denny's restaurant in silence. Catalina was waiting for them out front, bouncing up and down in tiny ballet flats. In her hands was a cardboard holder filled with three coffee cups.

"Hi, ladies!" she chirped as she hopped into the passenger seat. Her cheeks were pink and her eyes sparkled with excitement. She wore a bright green sweater with a blue flannel scarf draped around her neck. "Coffee?"

Catalina wore a scent similar to baby powder that mixed with the coffee. Already the mood in the van was picking up, at least for Elise. Sonya still stared sourly out the windshield.

"Thank you. I'd love some," Elise said. Catalina twisted in her seat to pass back the cup. Elise took a sip and tried to hide her grimace. Black wasn't her favorite, but beggars couldn't be choosers. "So, today is your final fitting then, right?" she began as a conversation starter.

"Yep! And we get to check out places for the wedding." Catalina squeezed her hands together, seemingly not able to contain her excitement.

"I think I have a tentative approval already on two of these venues," Sonya said. Her face was pale in the morning light, but her frown had disappeared. Maybe Catalina's energy was getting to her, too.

They pulled into an empty parking spot in front of Bride's Best bridal shop. Similar to the last time, the two women and their pet poodle greeted them at the door.

"Hello!" said Simone, this time wearing a baby blue dress suit.

"Hi, there," Elise responded, trying to get out of the way of Catalina, who plowed past her.

"Are you ready? Our seamstress just finished it last night! It looks gorgeous!" Allison trilled out. Despite the enthusiasm, Elise noted the bare movement of her face and decided she must be fresh from a dermatological visit. The two consultants ushered Catalina to the back room to help her change.

Sonya collapsed onto one of the couches in the viewing area. She looked over at Elise. The dog wandered over, and Elise offered her hand for the poodle to sniff. Cupcake sat elegantly next to the couch and blinked wise-appearing eyes. *If you could only have seen what I have seen*, those eyes seemed to say.

Elise stroked the dog's neck. "I told you we wouldn't be late."

"Oh, hush." Sonya spouted back. She pushed up the sleeve of her cream-colored cardigan to examine her newest tattoo. It was a Phoenix rising out of a sea of flames.

"Beautiful," Elise murmured, leaning over to get a better look.

Sonya smiled. "Just part of my story. Over here, I'm getting a magpie." She pointed to the back of her shoulder.

"You like birds?" Elise asked, curious.

"I used to have one air-brushed on my bike," she answered, glancing at the floor. She yanked down her sleeve with a pained look.

"What happened to your bike?"

There was a long pause—so long that Elise considered making some inane comment just to cut the awkwardness—before Sonya finally said, "Laid it out. Different lifestyle then. Different life." Sonya stood up and walked away, effectively cutting off any more conversation.

Well, that's interesting, but actually not too surprising. What is surprising is how a biker chick went from riding a motorcycle to driving a VW bus.

"Here she is!" Simone announced as if ushering the Queen of England. "Miss Beautiful, herself!" The dark-haired consultant swept back the curtains.

Catalina stood there with wide eyes as if she herself couldn't believe how wonderful she looked. The strapless dress highlighted her pale shoulders and slender collarbones. The dress fell to the floor, hiding the tops of her shoes. Standing there in the soft light, she did have an ethereal quality about her.

Carefully, she lifted the front and minced into the room.

"What do you think, ladies?" Allison asked. "Isn't she lovely?" As lovely as Catalina was, Elise admired the sincere awe that Allison interjected into her tone. After years of seeing women in wedding dresses, it was impressive how the consultant made it seem as though there had been none before the little blonde woman standing before them.

"She definitely is," Elise agree.

"Spin around," Sonya directed with a twirl of her finger. Catalina did an awkward rotation. Sonya frowned. "The dress is dragging on the ground. Are you wearing heels?"

Catalina shook her head. "Not today, just my flats."

"I don't understand?" Sonya shook her head in apparent confusion. "Every other time I've seen you, you've been wearing one sparkly pair or another."

"I'm not sure if that would be a great idea, seeing how clumsy I am recently." She ran the palm of her hand along the scrape on her forearm.

"Oh, sweetie, that was a terrible fall," Allison pressed her lips into a commiserating frown. She wouldn't make eye contact with Elise, presumably still offended by Elise asking for the names of the purchasers of the green shoes.

Sonya twisted her lips in deep thought. Finally, she shook her head. "Well, the dress is too long. The poor girl's going to trip on the way down the aisle." She came closer and touched the wedding dress waist. "And whose idea was it to put the boning in like this? Surely this isn't how it was designed."

"I'm going to need to take a break," Catalina said, looking anxiously from one consultant to the other.

"Honestly, this boning is much too tight," Sonya continued. "It looks like actual ribs. And the bodice is gaping. What are you trying to do?"

"Oh, surely it's not as bad as that," Allison started. She came over and fiddled with the bodice also.

"Sorry, guys, I need to use the..." Catalina began again.

"We were trying to keep it nicely fitted, while still allowing room..." Simone interjected.

"Room?" Sonya's eyebrows went up. "Room for what? The wedding cake?"

"You know," Allison dipped her head a couple of times in the direction of Catalina.

"Bathroom," Catalina whispered, before lunging for a purse. She opened it and quietly upchucked into the contents. Closing it, she wiped her mouth. "I'm so sorry about that."

Sonya blinked hard. She turned stiffly back to the wedding consultants. "I have this feeling I'm the last to know. Is she — ?"

"Pregnant." Catalina finished. "Yes, I am." She giggled and patted her stomach.

"Lovely," Sonya breathed. Gathering herself together, she nodded firmly. "Get this boning removed pronto. Have the seamstress use darts instead. Right now this poor woman looks like she's wearing a skeleton nightgown." She clasped her hands before her and continued matter-of-factly. "It needs to be hemmed by at least three inches. This poor girl does not need to worry about tripping along the aisle, especially now in her condition. And somebody clean out my purse."

The consultants leapt to the table. Simone returned with pins to mark the hem, while Allison ran to the bathroom with the purse.

When Sonya was satisfied with the way the alterations were ordered, she led the two other woman back out to the van. "One fire out, two more to go."

"Fires?" asked Catalina, pulling on her seatbelt. She pushed it under her belly with a sweet smile.

"When we're this close to the deadline, everything is on fire," Sonya explained, pulling out onto the road.

"Look!" Elise pointed. "There is that…." her voice trailed off. She watched behind her as the van sped forward.

"That what?" Catalina asked, trying to see what Elise was looking at.

"That girl. I've seen her around town lately."

"Oh. Her." Catalina's mouth pressed into two lines.

Startled at Catalina's response, Elise leaned forward. "Do you know her?"

Chapter 15

The van shuddered as Sonya shifted into third gear. "So, should I be expecting a shotgun at the wedding?" Sonya asked sarcastically as she turned the corner onto Main Street.

"A shotgun?"

"Yes. Your Uncle Rozzo isn't going to show up wielding one is he? To make sure Cook marries you?"

Catalina laughed. "No. Cook's more excited about this baby than I am." She rested her hand on her hardly-there tummy. "If that's even possible."

Sonya's van was so loud, Elise could barely hear. She leaned forward to ask, "Do you know if it's a boy or a girl?"

Catalina's earrings swung as she shook her head. "No. That won't be until next month. But we've heard the heart beat." Her face flashed with joy. "It was incredible, like a hamster drinking from its water bottle."

A hamster? This girl cracks me up. "Sweet," Elise smiled. Now that Catalina seemed to have simmered down, she asked again, "That girl back there. Do you know who she is?"

Catalina shrugged. "When you're a part of a circus, you attract runaways. She's one that's tried to tag along with us. Uncle Rozzo has threatened to call the cops on her more than a few times."

"I thought the circus hired kids like that? I don't mean that offensively," Elise amended hurriedly, "I guess it's just my impression. Maybe from TV shows or something."

"Runaways are always up to no good. They've stolen my shoes and clothing, and I caught that girl near my stuff recently. Besides, you start collecting kids and then the police get involved, and not in a good way. Most towns already have it in for us as it is. You can't even believe the names we get called."

"Aww, I'm so sorry." Elise winced, feeling uncomfortable. Bullying was something that hit her to the core, bringing back way too many memories from her own experiences in junior high.

"You're strong, I'm sure," Sonya said, flipping on her blinker. "You can't let what other people say have an on impact you. You have to define who you are and never let anyone dissuade you from that."

"Oh, I agree. And carnies are good at that. We're down with whatever it takes to defend our own too, but we don't borrow trouble where we don't need to." Catalina shrugged, looking unemotional about the homeless teen's fate in a way that made Elise's blood run cold. She eased back into her seat and looked out the window. *What is that girl running away from? She looked like she was starving, and now after hearing Catalina, it seems she really might be.*

Sonya turned again, this time into the parking lot of Angel Lake Park. "Okay, we're here. Let's get out and explore a bit."

The three of them climbed out. Sonya led the way down to the sandy beach. "You can't see it, but over there is a covered area where we can have the reception if you want. This can be the backdrop for your actual ceremony." Sonya gestured out to the lake. Today, the water was choppy with little white-capped waves. At the shore a small boy threw stones in the water, breaking into laughter at the "plunk" sound.

Catalina's face puckered with deep thought. She walked farther out onto the beach, sliding a bit as her shoes sank in the sand. One must have filled with sand because she took it off and shook it out. She wiggled her foot back in and continued down to the water.

With her hands on her hips, she scanned the area with a decidedly dubious look on her face.

"Well?" Elise said, slightly hopeful. "Isn't it gorgeous? It's one of my favorite places ever."

Catalina turned to her left where the breeze traveling over the water ruffled her hair. She crossed her arms at its coldness and shivered. Her earrings were shaking an adamant 'no' along with her head as she pivoted back to the women. "Nope. This is definitely not it." Without waiting for a response, Catalina stalked back up to the van, her ankles threatening to turn with every other step.

"Okay, then. Four days left and still no venue." Sonya said. She stared out at the lake. The breeze did little to move the blonde swoop of hair on top of her head, stiffened as it was with gel. She glanced at Elise, her eyes appearing an even paler gray than usual in the light. "I told you she was a Miss Priss." Slowly, she walked back up the beach to the van.

Elise blew out a big lungful of air and rubbed her arms. That darn air was freezing cold. Or maybe it was the company she was with. She couldn't be sure.

Why did I choose this job again?

Oh, yeah. I have bills to pay.

Ten minutes later, Sonya pulled into another parking lot. This park was obviously well loved by many kid's sports teams. The grass was torn up and muddy in places, with a baseball diamond taking half the field.

"Are you serious?" Catalina's eyes were huge as her head swiveled from looking out the window back to Sonya. "Uh. No way. I'm not even getting out." She sighed like a disgusted teenager.

"I told you the pickings were slim with this time frame." Sonya said, shifting the bus into park.

Catalina rolled her eyes. "Really? The backdrop is an abandoned factory. Probably alive with gangs and homeless people ready to head over for a free meal. Honestly, I'm disappointed."

Elise felt the mood of the van drop. Anger could almost be felt tangibly rising from Sonya's stiffened shoulders. "If you don't like the way I'm doing my job, we can discuss canceling the contract right now." Her voice was low and measured, with danger underlining every word.

It was a message Catalina received loud and clear. Immediately, she backed down and replaced the pouty look with her characteristic smile. "I'm sorry. Between the stress of Papa's health, me not feeling good, Cook leaving...." Her smile fell then as tears formed at the corners of her eyes. Angrily, she turned toward the window and hid her face. "Argh! I hate when I get like this."

Sonya softened too. "How is your dad doing?"

Catalina fanned her hands before her eyes and blew hard. "He's a fighter. Doing better than expected, really."

"You are going through a lot. You want a dream wedding, and I aim to provide it. I have one more place to try. It's kind of unconventional, but I think you're going to like it."

"Unconventional, huh?" Catalina settled back into her seat with a smile. "Sounds like my perfect place."

Chapter 16

Sonya pulled into the nearly empty shopping mall parking lot. Catalina raised an eyebrow but didn't say anything.

"Hold your opinion for just a minute," Sonya pleaded, holding her hands out in a calming motion. Catalina nodded as she rewound her scarf around her neck.

They walked up to the door. Elise saw a pair of faded motorized horses sitting by the door. A memory flashed of when she was a little girl riding on that very horse.

It was freezing outside. Elise bounced on her toes to keep warm while Sonya rifled through her purse for a set of keys.

"So, where was the circus performing before you came here?"

Catalina looked to the ground and mumbled the answer.

"Where?" Elise leaned forward to hear.

"Meadowford." Catalina was suddenly interested in a dandelion that had sprouted from a crack in the sidewalk.

Meadowford. Where have I heard that recently?

Shaking the key ring, Sonya gave a triumphant cry as she found the one she was looking for and unlocked the glass doors. It just took just a bit of pressure from her hands on the doors to open them, and they were soon in the mall.

"An abandoned shopping mall?" Catalina asked. Their footsteps echoed loudly in the empty arboretum.

"Not completely empty. There are a few businesses open during the week on the other end. But this right here," Sonya waved her hand around, "Is open to rental." She gave Catalina a serious look. "I know you were hoping for something outside, but I think this could really be it. Just think about it for a minute."

"What happened here? Why is it empty?" Catalina asked. She fiddled with the end of her scarf, bringing it up to her mouth.

"Online shopping, I suppose. It's the wave of the future. There's a furniture store and a jewelry store at the end. I guess people don't want to shop online for those." Sonya's normally stern eyes winked in a bit of sadness. "I remember spending the weekends at the mall with my friends in high school. We'd people watch, drink an Orange Julius. It's a shame. I wonder what teens do these days."

"Instagram, SnapChat," Elise said. "It really is a different world."

"Not so different," Catalina smiled. "Not while we still have the circus." She licked her bottom lip and jammed her hands in her pockets. Her head tipped up and she examined the large glass ceiling above them. She wandered slowly with a thoughtful look.

Three trees grew in a park-like oasis with a waterfall in the center. The water fell in a soft, tinkling pattern down the stone, not so loud as to be intrusive.

The floor was dark. At one point, there might have been tables bolted to the floor, but they were long removed, leaving the laminate covered in a pattern of circles.

Sonya stood back with her arms crossed and let Catalina take it all in. Elise walked around, too.

The area was large enough to hold a crowd comfortably. Four dark hallways radiated out from the center of the arboretum leading to various stores.

Catalina walked clear around the waterfall and made it back to Sonya. She wore a hint of a smile.

Sonya winked. "It's nice, huh?" The tall woman stepped back and stretched her hands before her as though describing a film set. "Imagine chairs leading up to the waterfall. An altar there, with white gardenias woven around a natural wood trellis. The pathway to the altar would be red velvet sprinkled with white rose petals from your flower girls. And here," Sonya gestured dramatically. "Would be your musical quartet playing the wedding hymn. Perhaps a singer? The acoustics in here are incredible." To demonstrate, she sang out a few bars of Adele's newest hit. Her husky, soft voice sounded incredible.

Through all of this, Catalina's face grew pinker and her smile stretched bigger.

"Down there," Sonya continued, "We'll have the buffet. There are kitchens in what was once the food court. We'll have our caterers use those. All the tables and chairs will be dressed up with linens, covers and flowers. Imagine tiny lights," here Sonya glanced at the ceiling, "streaming down from the ceiling." She looked boldly at Catalina, who seemed caught almost in a trance at the wedding planner's words. "You won't even recognize this place."

Catalina was nodding before Sonya even finished. "Yes! Yes!" She clapped her hands. "This is it. This truly is my dream wedding venue."

Sonya smiled confidently. She looked in her phone and quickly shot off a text. Two minutes later, her phone dinged. "And, it's yours." Sonya said with finality.

Elise was impressed. This was the reason why Sonya was the boss. In the ninth inning, her boss had found the exact right place, and procured both the bride-to-be's permission *and* the agreement with the establishment. Elise shook her head. *This is why Sonya gets the big bucks.*

Catalina spun in a circle, hugging herself. Her eyes glowed. "Are you serious? It's mine? I'm getting married here?"

"You are." Sonya said calmly. "And it's going to be amazing."

Catalina ripped her phone out of her purse and quickly dialed. After a moment, she let out a squeal. "Cook? Cook! I found the perfect place! Oh my gosh! You're going to love it! Oh baby, I love you so much. I can't wait to marry you, my little snookums."

With quick steps, Catalina walked behind the fountain to continue her affectionate conversation. Elise caught Sonya's eye and wrinkled her nose.

"Ahh, ahh," Sonya scolded. "It's what we're here for. Making the romance and magic happen."

"Snookums?"

"The sappier the better. That's how I know I've truly done my job. We take pride in making them melt into baby talk." Sonya raised her eyebrow with a smile.

"You really are amazing. I can't believe you just pulled this off."

Sonya shrugged. "After doing it for as long as I have, you get to read your clientele. It really isn't that hard. Sometimes, you have to maneuverer things around until you get them to want what they need. Make them think it's their idea." She waggled her fingers in the air. "Smoke and mirrors."

Catalina giggled loudly, and they watched her return. She clicked her phone away and dropped it into her shiny purse. "He's so excited!" Catalina smiled. "Just four more days! I can't wait!"

"We have a lot to do in that time," Sonya warned. "You did pick your cake options the other day with your Uncle? Did you finalize your menu options?"

"Yes, I filled out the menu at the caterers. There was so much yummy food it was hard to decide."

"But you did." Sonya deadpanned.

Catalina nodded.

"Did you follow the chef's suggestions, or…"

"Oh, we followed them," Catalina answered, before looking guiltily at the floor.

Sonya paused, subtly scratching her arm. Elise remembered the new tattoo. "It's okay to vary the menu somewhat, but you should have a general fare.

It's a reception, not a potluck. You want to pair together foods that will enhance each others' flavors."

"I decided on the complete menu the caterer suggested for the prime rib. I just added candy corn."

Sonya looked startled, as if she'd never heard of candy corn before.

"And Doritos." Catalina added, looking guilty.

Sonya rubbed her forehead. "Dear heavens, I sent a pregnant woman by herself to pick out the menu." She gave a big sigh. "Okay. I'll track down the chef and just have a little look-over at what he's serving. Will you trust my judgement if I find anything missing?"

"I really want the Doritos." Catalina said earnestly.

"I'll make sure you have them. But maybe after you change out of your white dress." Sonya gave a brittle smile. "Okay, ladies. Since this is concluded, let's get out of here so I can continue my job."

Chapter 17

After they dropped Catalina off back at Denny's, things really kicked into high gear back at the boutique. Sonya had two contractors that she worked with exclusively for the manual labor of setting up and tearing down the wedding venues. She was on the phone as soon as she walked through the door, her shucked sweater dangling haphazardly from where she'd tossed it on the coat tree. Relentlessly, she paced the boutique as she hammered out the details of assembling the trellis, rug rentals and stringing up lights.

Elise was on the other end of the room on her cell, one finger in her ear so that she could hear, attempting to locate and reserve chairs, linens, and a limousine rental.

Two hours later, they both had a break. Sonya glanced over at Elise and laughed. "Quite a bit of leg-work, eh? All right, I need to call the florist again. I'd put in an order last week but, like everything in the business world, you have to babysit, to make sure it's done correctly. Oh, that's right. I need to get a call in to the caterer." She rubbed her arm where her tattoo still seemed to itch. "Find out how messed up the menu is. Also, I need to decide where the bridal party will be getting ready." She tapped her paper. "Do we try to rent one of the empty stores down at the mall?" She picked up her phone to text. "I'll ask Catalina, but I think we need to get on the horn to the furniture rental company and get a couple couches, curtains, and mirrors to spruce the store up into a proper changing room." Sonya sent the text then watched the phone as if expecting an immediate answer. When it didn't come, she uncharacteristically slouched into one of the lounge chairs. Her face suddenly drooped wearily in a way that alarmed Elise.

"Hey, you doing okay?" Elise asked. "Can I get you some coffee? Water?"

The tall woman closed her eyes and shook her head. "Sometimes, this job gets to me."

"I hear you. It's pretty amazing, the work that you do. How long have you been a wedding planner? Is it something you've always wanted to do?"

Sonya's lips curved with a slight sardonic smile. "This wasn't my dream. My dream was to travel the world like a nomad. Never stopping, always discovering. Answer to no one. But instead, I found myself here."

Elise was shocked. Who would do this if they weren't driven? "You're kidding me? You're like a natural."

"I told you, I had a whole other life before this. I ended up totaling my Harley on Blewett Pass. Totally my fault, a rookie move, really." Her gaze traveled to the floor as her face grew even more somber.

"What happened?"

"Deer jumped out in front of me. I swerved, over-corrected. Wiped out. Ended up tweaking my shoulder so badly I couldn't hang on to the handlebars anymore." Her hand went up to massage the shoulder at the memory. "There went my big dreams of travel. My ol' man left me and suddenly I was alone, nearly forty, with no way out. I found this place for sale, and with the insurance money, I bought it. This was something I ended up being good at, so I'm here. But, I finally landed a job that's big enough to help get me out of here. That's been my goal all along." A hard glint came to her eyes.

"You mean the Petrovitsky wedding? So that's why you're so willing to put up with all the craziness."

"Exactly."

"What made you decide to buy a wedding boutique?"

"I figured if I wasn't going to have my own wedding, I'd help arrange others. Besides, the job called for a bossy woman who looks grouchy all the time if she's not smiling. My face was perfect for the job." Here, she laughed.

"Aw, you aren't the only one. I get asked what's wrong all the time, and I'll just be thinking about what I want for lunch." Elise smiled in return. Her stomach growled at the world *lunch,* which made both the women laugh harder.

"Why don't you run across the street and get us a couple sandwiches," Sonya said, climbing slowly to her feet. "It'll probably do us both some good. Do you mind doing that?"

"Not at all. What do you want?" Elise grabbed her purse from where she'd dumped it unceremoniously, on the ottoman when she'd first arrived.

"Turkey, avocado, light mayo. Here, use this." Sonya fished out a credit card and passed it over. "It's on me. Or rather, on the business."

Elise took the card and tucked it into her pocket. "Fries? Anything to drink?"

"Nope, that's all for me." Sonya was back on her phone again with her pen on her notepad. Elise quietly opened the door to keep the bells from chiming too hard.

The breeze was quick and knife-like across her bare legs below her skirt. *Dang, still cold.* Elise buttoned her business jacket and crossed her arms, shivering. She looked both ways as she waited for the traffic to clear. When it was apparent it wasn't going to let up, she resignedly walked up the block to use the crosswalk.

She hit the pedestrian button and waited, trying not to look like she was freezing. Straight across from her was the alley opening and, of course, her eye was drawn there again.

Her spine stiffened. This time, there was somebody in there. A dark shadow, bent over.

Waif-like.

The crosswalk bleeped a signal to say it was safe to cross. Elise jumped at the noise and then, blowing on her hands to warm them, hurried across the road.

She approached the alley's opening and squared her shoulders. *Just act confident.* Her steps were firm, heels clacking loudly on the sidewalk like she meant business. As she walked by, she gave it a quick perusal.

Her heart stopped in her throat. There she was. That little teenage girl, huddled down in a brown, ratty coat. Elise's steps slowed but the girl didn't look up. The teen's dark hair hung lankly across her face as she held her hands in her armpits.

"Hello," Elise called, hoping her voice sounded soothing. "I'm just going to get a bite to eat. Want to join me?"

The girl jumped and looked up. Her dark eyes looked like oversized pools in her pale face. She stared for a moment, as if not knowing how to respond.

"Turkey sandwich with bacon?" Elise added, hoping the sound of food would spur the teenager to movement.

The girl licked her lips and started to stand, jerking hesitantly as if she were a brand new foal making its first steps. She gripped the edges of her frayed jacket more tightly around her and shuffled out in hiking boots that looked a size too big.

Elise stepped back from the opening. "It's cold out here," she said quietly. "You'd never guess it was spring. By the way, my name's Elise."

After that first glance, the girl kept her eyes locked towards the ground. "Lucy," she mumbled.

"Hi, Lucy. You like bacon?"

Lucy flinched, as if shying away from the question. *Okay, no questions then.* Elise gripped the cold handles of Kelli's Diner and opened the door. "Well I like bacon, and I'm ordering extra. You can too."

The girl's glance skated quickly over Elise's face. She nodded and tucked her hair behind her ears.

Elise produced the credit card from her pocket. "My boss's treat," she whispered conspiratorially.

They stood by the counter waiting to be seated. A waitress came over with a big grin that faltered slightly at the sight of Lucy. She hesitated with the menus until Elise urged, "We'd like to sit down."

With her grin turned up again, the waitress nodded. "Right this way." She led them to a booth in the far back, away from the other customers.

Elise sat on one side, with Lucy on the other. The waitress placed their menus before them, saying with a southern twang, "I'll be right back with some water. Ya'll want some sweet tea?"

Elise looked over for a response, but Lucy had buried her face in the menu as if trying to hide. "Not right now, thank you," Elise said. "Actually, maybe some hot tea instead."

The waitress nodded and walked away, hips swaying.

"Okay," Elise started, trying to keep the atmosphere light. "You see anything you like? Hamburger? Sandwich?"

"I'd like some pancakes," the girl's voice sounded raspy, as if she hadn't spoken in a while.

"Pancakes?" Elise searched for them on the menu and found them. "You want bacon with that? Sausage?"

Lucy nodded, not indicating which one.

"Okay then," Elise said, shutting the menu. "We'll have both."

The waitress returned with a tray that held two white ceramic teapots, a container full of tea bags, and two coffee cups. She arranged the items on the table and then reached for her pad from her apron pocket. "What can I get ya'll?"

"I'd like a turkey sandwich with avocado, light on mayo to go. And then a turkey club for me, and a stack of pancakes with a side of both bacon and sausage for my friend."

The waitress glanced warily at Lucy, but wrote it down. She scooped up the tray and the menus, saying "Okay, that should be out shortly," as she turned to go.

Well. Now what? Without menus to distract them, the silence seemed to be even more awkward. Elise entwined her fingers and rested her hands on the table. She found herself studying the teen. *Don't look at her and freak her out.* Quickly, she glanced out the window.

"You don't have to ignore me. I don't bite," Lucy mumbled. "And I might be able to help you, too." She reached for the sugar packets and laid them out in front of her as though they were a deck of cards. One by one, they disappeared into her pocket.

"I don't think you'll bite. You think you can help me?" Elise was instantly curious.

"I know things." Lucy spun the spoon in a lazy circle on the table.

"Like what?"

The teenager shrugged. "Secrets. Like maybe about the Craigslist Bandits."

"Is it gossip from the circus? You've been trying to get on with them, right?"

Lucy jerked in the seat as if she were about to bolt.

"No, wait. I'm not going to say anything. Or do anything," Elise quickly amended. She held her hands up, and again tried to speak soothingly. "You don't have to talk with me. Just eat your food and then go, if that's what you want."

Slowly, the teen settled back in the seat. She eyed Elise warily, then went back to the sugar packets, picking the bowl clean, until none remained. Soon, the tea bags had disappeared too.

The waitress returned with two plates of food before leaving again. On her return trip she had syrup, butter and a styrofoam container of what Elise assumed was the turkey sandwich. Quietly, the two dug in. Elise watched under hooded eyes with fascination as Lucy used every bit of butter and then flooded the plate with syrup. She also noticed the napkins were missing from the table, probably squirreled away too, and scooted to the next table to remove the ones sitting there.

They both made quick work of their meals. Lucy ate everything, using the last bite of pancake to finish mopping up the syrup. She drank her tea and slowly melted back against the padded booth with a sigh. She glanced up at Elise and graced her with a smile.

Elise smiled back, feeling her heart squeeze. This was her first real look at the girl, and she appeared no older than fifteen. Her face was dirty, but still held some of the baby fat of girlhood. "Is there anything I can do for you? Any place I can take you?"

Lucy shook her head and stood up. "Thank you for the food," she murmured, with another smile.

Bundling her jacket around her, she headed to the restroom. Elise watched her disappear inside and blew out a big breath. *Wow, that was interesting. What am I supposed to do now? Just let the poor girl go on her merry way? Who can help her? The street is no place for a girl like her.* She closed her eyes, feeling overwhelmed by a tidal wave of both sadness and helplessness. When she opened them again, Lucy was just passing by on her way to the exit.

"Lucy," Elise called and reached out her hand. Too late. The teenager was already through the front door and running down the sidewalk.

After Lucy had left, Elise went into the bathroom to clean up. As she washed her hands, she stared at her reflection. "Well, that was like trying to feed a stray dog. One wrong move and the dog takes off." She made a face at herself and shook the water off her hands. Still staring in the mirror, she suddenly froze.

Slowly she turned to look behind her. There, hanging off the stall's door by one elastic strap, was a white painter's mask.

Chapter 18

Elise reached for the painter's mask and untangled it from the metal door. *What does this mean? Had Lucy left it?* Elise found it hard to believe that it had been hanging there all this time since the robbery. What if it was some weird coincidence and someone was actually painting here in the restaurant?

That can't be right.

Back at the bridal shop, Sonya was still on the phone. She held it against her chest as Elise walked in. "Took you long enough." Sonya glanced at the mask in Elise's hands. "What's that?"

"Oh, I'm sorry. I met this homeless girl and ended up getting her a meal. I'll pay you back."

"No worries." Sonya took her styrofoam container. "But what do you have there?"

"I found it in the bathroom. I want to show Brad." " Elise laughed, realizing how silly it sounded. "I mean, it's probably nothing, but weird right?" She held the mask back and studied it. "Man, that was a scary day."

Sonya nodded and returned to her call. "Yes. That's right." She carried her sandwich with her into her office and shut the door.

Great. Now what?

Elise hadn't needed to worry. There at her desk was a list written in Sonya's cramped handwriting. She sat in the chair, making it squeak in protest, and read the first one.

1) Get your rear to Divinity flowers on 3rd. The florist screwed up the order and we have 4000 green carnations. Find out what flower is in season that she can get abundantly in white.

Elise realized this was the second mistake the florist had made in two weeks as she remembered the juggling act of wedding fiasco number one. *Green Carnations? Who'd order those?*

She scanned to number 2.

2) Call Cozy Clippers and beg, grovel, or offer your first born to convince them we need a stylist early Saturday morning. Peggy canceled, citing PTSD or something. If they say no, FIND ONE.

3) Keep an eye on your email. I put up a Craigslist ad for people to help us set it up. Ronnie, our normal construction guy, has the flu- typical of a man. I've emailed you a few questions to ask the applicants. If they seem reputable, Hire them!

Elise turned the paper over to discover the list continued down the back side. She sighed and searched up the number of Cozy Clippers and dialed them.

"Hello!" a bright voice answered. "How can I help you today?"

"Hi, there. I'd like to schedule a beautician for a wedding on Saturday."

The voice was immediately cautious. "What time will she be needed?"

"Umm," Sonya hadn't written that down on her list. "I'm thinking at seven am?"

"Is this for the Petrovitsky wedding?"

Whoa. How did they know? "Yes?"

"I'm sorry. We're booked at that time."

"Well, hang on a second. We had confirmation from you that one of your beauticians was committed to being there. She backed out at the last second."

"She backed out because she doesn't want to be held responsible for anything happening to that woman's hair. And frankly, no one else here is interested in working with *carnies*." The last word sounded like it had been spit out.

Elise blinked hard. Seriously? "That doesn't seem very professional. In fact, it seems quite judgmental...." The phone line went dead. Sighing, she grabbed her keys and headed out for the florist.

*** ***

"You can't do anything?" Elise looked with amazement at the middle-aged florist. The florist raised her eyebrows and lightly shrugged. "That's what the order said." She flapped the paper at Elise. "Four thousand green carnations."

"That doesn't even make sense. Who took the order?" Elise asked. She was flabbergasted at even having this discussion.

The woman's cheeks flushed. She answered, sounding a little huffy, "My assistant, Patrick. But that doesn't matter. He's been here nearly a year and he absolutely knows how to take an order."

Elise raised her eyebrow. "When you saw this, didn't you consider that there could have been some misunderstanding? I mean, who in their right mind would order this many green carnations for a wedding?"

The florist crossed her arms, clearly done with this conversation. "You'd be surprised what people order. And don't be thinking you're getting out of paying for the flowers. You make sure you let your boss know. You aren't sticking me with the bill for all of these carnations."

"Well, I'd think after the last mistake at the wedding two weeks ago, you would have wanted to double check this time."

"That wasn't my fault. I told Sonya it was hard to get lilies of the valley at this time of year, and we'd better have a substitute. She's very headstrong. It was lucky I went ahead and had the Dendrobium Orchids on hand just in case."

Elise nodded. It was true. Sonya didn't take 'no' from anyone, not even Mother Nature. "All right, I'll let her know what happened."

At the door, Elise paused then turned around. "Does it say on the form who called in the order?"

❁ ❁ ❁

"Catalina." Sonya growled out. "I'm going to kill her. Why would she do that? Why would she insist she wanted hydrangeas and calla lilies, only to order four thousand green carnations? Who even does that?"

Elise shook her head, then remember Sonya couldn't see her on the cell phone. She'd dreaded facing Sonya and so had called her instead to inform her of the news. Her soft voice was much easier to deal with than her menacing scowl.

"So what do you want me to do?" Elise asked.

"Well, that woman's going to be having carnations for her wedding." Sonya bit off each word. "I'll give Catalina a call and talk with her myself."

Elise cleared her throat. "Okay. I'm still on the hunt for a hair dresser."

Issuing a string of curses, Sonya hung up.

That was...pleasant.

Before she could tackle anything else, she sent out an emergency text.

Brad, please tell me you're coming over tonight.

Man, she was really falling for that man. Just thinking about him made her heart hurt in the best way.

He texted back promptly like she knew he would.

You better believe it, baby.

A smile crossed her mouth. She then sent a text to her best friend.

EEE

It was their code to announce an emergency that had carried over from high school.

Like Brad, Lavina's text was immediate. **I'm at home. Come over and I'll give you some sweet tea. Or wine. I have both. And if Brad did anything to you, he's gonna get it.**

Chapter 19

"Hello, darlin'." Lavina's front door was open and she was leaning out, waiting for Elise to show up. As usual, she was impeccably dressed in fitted pants and a silk blouse. Not to mention high heels. Lavina never went anywhere without them.

Elise smiled gratefully at her friend, but as she walked inside, her stomach was in knots.

"Good heavens. What's wrong with you? You look like a puppy who just learned he's about to be neutered."

Despite how she felt, Elise laughed. "That doesn't even make sense. A dog can't possibly know what that means."

Lavina sat down in her wingback chair and crossed her legs. "You ever take a dog to the vets to get fixed?"

Elise shook her head.

"Then you don't know. There's some weird doggy intuition right there. When we took in Claude, our Saint Bernard, it took five of us just to get him out of the truck."

Elise nodded, convinced. She actually felt like it would take five people just to get her to return to her job.

"So, what's the matter. Is this a job for sweet tea or wine?"

"Neither. I originally came because I needed some help tracking down a beautician, but on my way here, I received this." Elise turned her phone toward Lavina so her friend could read.

Don't plan on getting any sleep tonight. I need you.

"Well that might not be so bad, depending on who it's from. Brad, maybe?" She raised a penciled-in eyebrow.

Elise snorted. "It's from my boss, Sonya. It turns out I've chosen a terrible career path to walk on."

"Path?"

"This darn job! I thought it was going to be so sweet and nice. I think subconsciously I pictured a lot of cake tasting and consoling brides that everything was going to be okay. Instead, I'm a ball of stress trying to deal with all of this."

Lavina smiled calmly. "Don't you worry your pea picking head about any of this. I know this is gonna work out. Maybe we can crumble up some Valium and put it on top of the cupcakes. You have a tasting later today don't you?"

A laugh busted out of Elise. "No, that was a while ago. Anyway, it's my boss that's the problem more than the bride." She looked at Lavina. "Why don't you just hire me?"

Lavina's made a slight wince. She stood up slowly, "Wine it is. Now, Elise, you know I love you, but I'm afraid to work together where there are knives available. One of us might possibly stab the other."

"Vi!"

"I'm just saying we've had our heated squabbles through the years. It's better if pointy utensils aren't close at hand."

"I can't have wine. I'm on the clock for who knows how long." Elise thought about missing Brad that night and covered her face. "Ugh. My life."

Lavina returned with a plate of macarons and a pitcher of tea. "Well, have this then. Now, what were you saying about a beautician?"

Quickly, Elise filled her in on the hairdresser problem. "And I have to figure out what to do with four thousand green carnations. Who would even do something like that?"

"Well, green is lucky. Maybe that young bride felt like she could use some luck right about now. And possibly she was afraid to ask for them herself."

Wrinkling her brow, Elise thought back on Catalina's hard reaction at the sight of the second venue. "No, I don't think so. She's very sweet, but there definitely is a hidden side to her. I think she'd cut a girl."

Fluffing her red hair off her shoulder, Lavina laughed. "Listen to you. Well, maybe there's another reason. Maybe she feels confident that she can go over Sonya's head. After all, she's the one footing the bill."

Elise nodded. "Maybe that was it. But who would want carnations?"

With a cool shrug, Lavina poured the tea. "Maybe she likes green. Maybe they have some weird meaning for her. In the mean time, let me call my gal and see if she's free on Saturday morning."

"I'd really appreciate it. Or at least, give me a direction on who to call."

"Why didn't you call your gal?"

"I'm not sure that a place that gives ten dollar haircuts is exactly the quality Sonya is looking for. And I sure as heck don't want to disappoint her."

Lavina laughed. "Ten dollars? It costs more to take a dog to the groomers."

"Hey! Watch it. I'm still trying to get back on my feet."

"I'm sorry, so sorry." Lavina held her hands up. "You are doing a good job. Next year though, when you're in a better place, we're giving your beautician an upgrade." She pulled out her cell and dialed the number. Her face was serene as she waited for someone to answer. Then, as if hit by electricity, her face animated with a huge smile. "Tabitha, darlin'? It's Lavina. How are you?" The voice on the other end rippled through the earpiece in equal animation and excitement. Lavina listened for a moment, nodding. "Was that red carpet to die for? Absolutely the best fund raiser I've been to all year. Could you believe *she* showed up with *him*?" More laughter ensued from the both of them.

Elise sat and watched, half impatient to find out the answer, half in amusement to see her friend act like such a socialite. Her eyes narrowed. *Wait a minute... Vi really is a socialite.* She sighed and took another drink of her tea. *Life is becoming a bit too weird lately.*

"Well, darlin', the reason I called is that I have a horrid favor to ask of you. My very best friend, Elise

—do you remember her? Yes, I do need to bring her in to let you do your magic—anyway, she's in a desperate search for the most amazing beautician to help with a wedding party on Saturday."

Lavina's comments dissolved into a few mmhmm's. Elise ran her fingers through her shoulder length hair, a bit nonplussed. *What's wrong with my hair?*

"Oh, really, darlin'? Oh, she will be *so* pleased." Lavina flashed a thumbs up. "Yes, let me just get you her number. I may pop in, too, to give a hand. Okay, I'll see you then!"

Lavina smiled as she rang off. "So, there you go." She reached for a macaron and popped it into her mouth.

"Thank you so much. I was seriously thinking I was going to have to kidnap someone."

"Kidnapping, huh? Well, you know what my Grandmama used to always say," Lavina raised an eyebrow looking wise.

"What?"

"Don't do something during the day time that will keep you awake at night."

Elise smiled, remembering the old woman. She always wore an apron and had just the pinkest cheeks. "Your grandma was wise. Plus, the hairdresser would be trying to get away and stuff."

Lavina nodded sagely. "Unless you decided to off them."

Elise choked on her cookie. "Too far, Vi, too far."

Chapter 20

T-minus 2. It was eight in the morning when Elise finally straggled back home. Sonya wasn't joking and had kept Elise up all night long assembling candle holders, place cards, and counting and ironing tablecloths. She decorated the toasting flutes, the unity candle, and cake servers. Even as of this morning, she was on the phone making sure all the deliveries, including the lattice archway, flowers, and cake would be on time.

Sonya had taken over hiring more workers to be at the venue to decorate, and they were arriving today. Her boss had sent her home to sleep, telling her to keep her phone next to her. "I'll call you when I need you," she'd said, her hair still swooped back exquisitely in its wave on the top of her head.

Elise left, feeling like a dog who'd spent the night rolling in a soggy heap in the yard. She checked her face in the car's mirror and rubbed under her eyes. "I have bills to pay," she reminded herself, before snapping the mirror back up.

She unlocked her front door to discover Brad asleep on her couch. He opened one eye and his arms to welcome her. She walked over, dropping her purse, and collapsed next to him.

"Hey, baby," he whispered.

"Don't smell me. Don't look at me. I am disgusting right now and feel like a zombie. But my heavens, I sure needed this."

His arms squeezed tighter around her and he kissed her head as she buried into the warmth of his chest.

"You're the best looking zombie I've ever seen."

Elise smiled. "It's just too bad for you."

"What is?"

She snuggled in a little deeper "If you only could market your hugs, you'd make millions of dollars. These are more calming and soothing than anything on the prescription market."

Brad laughed. "Lucky you, then."

"Any more word on the Craigslist Bandits?"

"Yeah. An informant told us that the bandits haven't left town."

Her eyes flickered a tiny bit at the news, but the comfort of his arms was too great. Exhausted, she fell asleep with him gently caressing her back.

❊❊❊

The next thing she knew, she was teetering on the edge of a mountain created by green carnations. Miles and miles of carnations as far as she could see. Everything was green. Down at the bottom, a tiny Sonya and Catalina yelled at her to make the flowers work. They turned into ants and crawled on her face trying to get in her mouth.

She awoke with a start. No. It was just Max tickling her face with his whiskers as he sniffed her nose. Her heart pounded as she glanced around. The living room was bright with the afternoon sun. Groaning, she sat up and stretched.

The scent of bacon hit her, making her feel human for the first time in a while. She arched her back and rubbed her face. Max had jumped from the couch and was immediately underfoot as she stood to her feet and stumbled to the bathroom.

The vision greeting her in the mirror was as bad as she thought. "Brainsss…" she muttered in her best zombie voice. She scrubbed her face clean and brushed her hair and teeth. Another check in the mirror proved that nothing else was going to help but a shower.

She hurried into her room for a clean t-shirt and wandered into the kitchen.

Brad stood in front of a sizzling frying pan with a dish towel tucked into his pants. "Hey, baby."

"Oh, my gosh. I can't believe how late I slept. And that smells so..." her eye caught the package of turkey bacon on the counter. "Turkey bacon! Why would you bring that travesty into my house?"

Brad laughed. "You're going to love it." He flipped a piece over with a fork.

"I'm not going to love it," Elise said doubtfully. "I barely like eggs, and only if they're covered in salsa. I eat eggs so I have an excuse to eat bacon."

"Why don't you just eat bacon by itself, if you don't like eggs?"

"There are rules to follow," Elise raised her eyebrows. "The same rules that involve saying 'no' to turkey bacon."

He winked at her. "Just give it a chance and see what you think."

Elise closed her eyes. "You're going to make me do this, aren't you?"

"Can't be afraid to try new things."

"I'm not afraid to try new things..."

Brad looked at her triumphantly.

"That I know I'll like!" she amended loudly as she scooped up Max.

"Have some coffee. Maybe that will help."

"I'll be fine. Just give me a minute to collect myself here," she responded. "Fake bacon is kind a blow."

He laughed and rifled through a cupboard for a plate. "Let me work my magic."

His voice was low and sexy and she couldn't keep the smile from her face. She buried her face into Max's fur. *I'm the luckiest girl in the whole world.*

"Tell me about Catalina. How'd it go?" he asked, cracking a few eggs in a pan.

"I like her. I'm not usually good with passionate people, but she's fun. She only experiences extreme feelings. Like she's devastated about the venue, but adores the cakes and Doritos. She cracks me up."

She sipped her coffee and continued. "There's only one thing that bothers me about her. There's this runaway teenage girl that hangs around the circus. Catalina just wants her gone; she's not interested in the poor girl's welfare."

"Really?" Brad frowned and dished up two plates. He had hidden hash browns, warming in the oven. Without being asked, he returned from the fridge with the salsa and set it on the counter next to Elise. "How do you know about the girl?"

Elise stared at the salsa and then looked up at Brad. "Come here," she said, reaching to hug him. "Thank you."

He kissed her, long and slow. "Hey, I've worked through the night a few times. I know how it goes. Now eat up."

"So about the girl. Her name is Lucy."

"Lucy, huh? Why am I not surprised you know."

"I saw her the other day in the alley."

"Which alley?"

"The one by the jewelers."

He arched an eyebrow.

"I can't help it if there's a lot of action happening around there lately." Elise bit into the bacon. *Hmm. Not bad. Not real good either, but not bad.* "Anyway, I offered her a sandwich and we talked. Honestly, I wish I could have helped her more, but she ran away." She gave Brad a guilty look. "So much has happened lately, I forgot to tell you about the painter's mask."

He paused with the fork half-way to his mouth. With a sigh, he set the fork down and waited. Elise recognized the tactic right away—his patented, "I'll just wait until you say something." She'd seen him do it before with suspects.

"I mean it. It was an accident!"

He took a sip of coffee and nodded.

"It was hanging in the bathroom of the diner."

"The same diner the waitress disappeared from."

"It's across the street from my work." She was a little put-out.

"I know, I know. I just have this weird feeling that even if it was across town, somehow you'd find your way there."

Elise took another bite of bacon to avoid answering.

"So you think the girl left it? Lucy?"

"I can't see any other way it would have gotten there. She mentioned she could help me." She shrugged. This bacon wasn't getting better.

"Where is it now?"

"In the trunk of my car."

"Covered in fingerprints," he finished.

"Ugh. I'm sorry. Again."

He shook his head. "I just wish you could be there to hear how I have to word this, time and time again, to our chief. He's either going to demand I arrest you for tampering, or he's going to deputize you and arrest me."

"I'm really sorry." She widened her eyes in her most innocent look.

Brad snorted and crunched on a piece of bacon. He tossed it back on the plate with a grimace. "This really isn't that good, is it?"

Chapter 21

At three o'clock Elise got her expected text. She was actually surprised Sonya had waited so long. It was short and succinct.

Meet me at the mall ASAP

"Time for me to go," she informed Max. Brad had left for work an hour earlier and she'd been lazing on the couch watching Friends reruns. Staying awake all night had taken its toll and her body felt like she'd been beaten up with a two by four.

Standing in her doorway, she looked back at the inside of her house. She didn't want to leave. Warm light spilled from the windows and splashed on the honey-wood floors. Max was perched up on the forbidden china cabinet. The couch was a hand-me-down and draped in colorful throw blankets. My home is cozy. Safe. *I'm doing this job so I can live here.*

She backed out of the driveway and turned onto the street. Her head was still sleepy. *I need to get some coffee.* Suddenly her eyes sprang open. Passing her on the other side was the beat-up green car. She watched in her mirror to see it hit its tail lights as it passed her house.

Goosebumps trickled up her spine. The green car didn't stop but continued on like it had the last time.

Elise turned the corner feeling shaky and sick. He *was* watching her. Thinking back to their conversation, she recalled him saying he had a new job. But who was *he*?

And who had given him the job?

There was nothing for it. She had to call Brad and let him know. Maybe he'd seen the green car around too.

At the stop sign, she quickly dialed. She grimaced as it went straight to voice mail. "Brad, this is your troublemaker. Listen," she cringed, "I forgot to let you know that this weird guy in a green car has been watching my house. Today is the second time I've seen him drive by. Maybe it's just a coincidence, but anyway. We can talk about it later. Have a good day, hon." She hung up.

There. At least that was done. *Maybe I'll ask Catalina if she knows who he is.* She sped toward the mall, more excited than ever to get this wedding done.

She parked her car and achingly walked across the parking lot. A van was there with the back rolled up. What is it with these white vans? This one had a giant flower on the side. Inside, two men grunted and manhandled tubs of green carnations down with the trolley.

Elise yanked open the door to the mall only to stop, paralyzed. All she could see was stack upon stack of boxes. *How in the world is this going to be a gorgeous wedding venue by tomorrow?*

Every muscle in her body clenched in protest at the work ahead. She sucked in a breath and pushed forward. Most of the action was around the fountain. Men, presumably hired from Craigslist, wobbled on tall ladders to hang lights. Sonya watched from below with her hands on her hips. She wore a white t-shirt with her tattoos all exposed. "Over there more," she directed.

Elise maneuvered around a set of planters and a giant rolled rug. "H-hi," she called hesitantly.

Sonya wheeled around until she spotted her. "Hi!" Sonya lifted her hand in greeting. She smiled as she walked over, more chipper than Elise had ever seen her. "Did you get some sleep?"

"Yeah, and you?"

"Oh, I napped in the other room for a little bit. There's just too much to finish up for any real sleep for me."

Elise numbly nodded. *What is she, a robot?*

"Come on, let me show you what we have left to get together." Sonya strutted ahead down the left hall, never questioning if she'd be followed.

And follow her, Elise did, like a puppy at the heels of his owner, hurrying to keep up. Sonya pointed to a business that once sold shoes. "In here," she pointed. Elise opened the door to discover even more boxes. "This is the beauty salon. The furniture will arrive tonight, so we'll need to get this room ready."

Elise spent the next couple of hours unpacking the boxes. Each unpacked box was set out in the hall, where it mysteriously disappeared, most likely stored away by one of the other workers.

Sonya came to check on her around dinner time. "This looks good," she said looking around. "I've ordered pizza, and there's a ton. Come have some and then I'll set you on your next task."

Elise had high hopes as she followed Sonya back, but the arboretum was still a madhouse. "Don't worry," Sonya said calmly. "This all really will come together. It has to." The last words were spoken fiercely.

A makeshift table had been set up and was covered with pizza boxes. It also was surrounded by workers. Elise walked over. Several of them stepped out of the way so that she could grab a slice. She took a bite, all the while looking for Sonya. Sure enough, there was her boss, tapping her foot. Elise walked over with the pizza. "Have you eaten?"

Sonya nodded. "Earlier. You ready to see your next task or do you need to finish…"

"No, show me. I can bring this along."

A voice stopped them in their tracks. "Hey, hey! How are things going?" Uncle Rozzo strutted through the door and pulled on the lapels of his jacket. Sonya rolled her eyes before turning around to face him. "Mr. Petrovitsky, what a surprise."

"Well, I've just come from the rehearsal and wanted to check in."

The tall woman smiled with the humor of an iceberg. "I'll be happy to answer your questions. Just let me get my assistant on her next task."

"Sure, sure. You go right ahead." He poked his fingers into one of the boxes to see inside.

Sonya spun around and strode down the opposite hallway, her jaw muscles jumping. This time she led Elise to the food court where another forest of boxes awaited.

Elise bit back a whimper.

"Start here," Sonya directed to a box of table linens. "Once you get the tables covered, start with the chairs. I'll send someone to help." Then she paused before turning back to Elise. "I keep seeing him."

"Who?"

"Rozzo. Let me know if he does anything weird. I don't like how he's lurking around." Her soft voice went even lower. "I don't care how nice Catalina is, you know how carnies are." Sonya gave a firm nod to make sure Elise understood her, and stalked away.

Elise's head throbbed. *Lovely. There's a mountain of work and suddenly my boss is paranoid on top of being a perfectionist and crazy.* She surveyed the tables and rubbed her temples. *Almost over. I can do this.* From the Panda restaurant came voices, and then loud laughter. She walked over and peeked in.

The back kitchen was filled with caterers preparing for the reception tomorrow. Ice chests and boxes lined the walls, with the counter filled with silver tureens and china dishes. One of the women looked up. "Hi! Are you working with us?"

Elise shook her head. "Sorry. No, I work for Sonya." At her boss's name, the woman made a face. The other caterers laughed.

"What's so funny?" Elise asked. *Great, what did Sonya do?*

"Let's just say she has quite the reputation."

Elise nodded, suddenly feeling uncomfortable. "Okay. Well, I'll be out here if you need anything." She turned back to the dining area and the task of dressing the tables.

She was delighted to see a familiar face. "Tanya!"

The dark haired woman who was bent over a box turned around. "Oh my goodness! You remember me?"

"Yep. You're the good news, bad news lady."

Tanya smiled and shook out a tablecloth. "How's it been going? She's a work horse, that's for sure."

"I'd call her a tyrant!" called a voice from one of the caterers.

Tanya laughed and widened her eyes. "I'd never say that in her hearing. I've seen her punch a contractor right in the face. That woman scares me."

Elise felt her eyebrows lift at the news. She grabbed a tablecloth and shook it out. She suddenly had the energy to really kick it into gear.

In the next few hours, they really made a difference to the dining area. Every table and chair was covered. Elise and Tanya were unwrapping the tables' center pieces when Sonya showed up.

"Just leave those in the box," she directed when she saw what they were doing. "I need the men to come in here and hang lights and I don't want them broken." With her arms crossed, she surveyed the room with a satisfied smile. "It's coming together. Good work, ladies." Then addressing Elise, "I just have one more thing for you to do. Come back out and help us set up chairs."

Elise straightened from where she'd been crouching by the last box. Her thighs felt shaky, reminiscent of when she'd finished her race. *How in the world is this woman going so strong?*

The arboretum was finally shaping up. Half the boxes had disappeared, instead replaced by two huge carts of chairs. Two men pulled the chairs off the stack. Elise joined the crew in carrying them to rows designated by chalk lines. Up in front more people worked on the flowers and assembled the trellis.

After another hour and half all three hundred chairs had been set up with the rug ready to be rolled up the aisleway.

Sonya walked up and squeezed Elise's shoulder. "Go home. Take some of that pizza with you. I'll see you by nine tomorrow."

Gratefully, Elise carried a box of pizza out to her car and dropped into her seat. *One more day. Just one more day.*

As she pulled out of the parking lot she saw the green car again. This time it was parked, and the driver was standing by its bumper talking with someone.

She drove by slowly, half wanting to duck, half needing to see.

The man turned his head and his face was illuminated by the streetlight.

Uncle Rozzo.

Elise gulped and slammed on the gas. Her skin prickled as though a bucket of ice water had been dumped on her.

What do I do? She grabbed her phone before chucking it, frustrated. Brad was still at work and hadn't responded to her message yet. *Do I go home?* The idea creeped her out. She drove around aimlessly, amped up on adrenaline.

After fifteen minutes she found herself outside Angel Lake Park. She stared at the sign illuminated by her headlights and gave a sarcastic snort. This place was her refuge, even after all these years. Whenever she had a puzzle to work out, she often found herself here. She turned the car off and sat in the dark. If she concentrated, she could just make out the moonlit ripples of the water between the trees.

She sat forward. There was something else moving between the trees. A person. Elise's creeped-out meter had hit its max and she jammed the keys in, ready to tear out of there. Something stopped her, and she leaned forward to watch some more.

The figure was slender. Tiny.

Waif-like.

Elise grabbed her jacket from the back seat and opened the door. "Lucy?" she called. The sound of her own voice made her pulse ramp up.

The figure turned toward her for a moment before ducking away. But not before Elise had a chance to see the thin face with the large eyes.

"Lucy! It's me, Elise." She looked desperately in her car. "I have some food for you!"

As the minutes passed it became apparent the teen wasn't coming forward. "Okay, I'm leaving now. The food will be by the sign." There was no indication that she'd been heard. *It's freezing out here. If only I could get her to come home with me.* With a sigh, Elise placed the pizza and the jacket on the ground. Feeling bummed out, she slowly drove away.

Chapter 22

Wedding day. Elise had awakened that morning with the biggest feeling of relief, as though waking from a nightmare. As she stretched in her bed, some of the previous day's events flashed through her mind — Lucy sleeping in the freezing cold. The creepy man driving by her house. She sighed and sat up. *I can only tackle it, one thing at a time.*

After her shower, she pulled her dress suit from the closet and wrinkled her nose at a stain she hadn't noticed on the edge of the skirt. *Frosting. Lovely.* She dabbed at it with a wet wash cloth and put it on. A quick chignon, a few swipes of mascara, and a granola bar, saw her out the door.

The parking lot was half-way full with two attendants dressed in full clown gear directing traffic. Elise followed the direction of one, and soon had the Pinto pulled into an empty spot. It was early yet, but Catalina's limousine was already there. Elise frowned, having expected to beat the bride-to-be.

She grabbed her jacket and shoved the remaining bit of granola bar into her mouth. Chewing, she checked her hair and then her teeth before climbing out.

The morning air was cool, but the clear sky overhead promised a beautiful day. Trees planted at the ends of the parking medians were unfurling baby leaves, as crocuses pushed through the dirt at the bases of their trunks.

A smile crossed her lips, despite her growing concern that something was bound to go wrong. *Think positive! Hopefully it'll just be something as simple as the wrong wedding cake topper.*

In the meantime, she had a job to do; to make this the best darn circus wedding that there ever was. She walked up to the entrance with a smile of approval. It was already shaping up to be a success. Green carpet lined the walkway up to the entrance, where two more clowns in white gloves stood to open the glass doors.

Elise gasped when she walked through the mall doors. The crew had obviously worked well into the night, transforming the mall's arboretum into a truly fairy tale scene. The waterfall was softly lit with green and golden lights. A blanket of woven carnations wrapped around its rock base. The flowers looked moss-like, instead of being the blaring colors of a football team that Elise had been expecting.

The workers had succeeded in assembling a white latticed trellis to arch over the wedding ceremony. Tiny lights twinkled amidst white trailing flowers woven in the wood framework.

There was definitely circus flair in there too. The carpet in the aisle separating the bride's family from the groom's was striped with shades of red, blue and green. Two giant urns, also painted in colorful stripes, were filled with white hydrangeas. The four exits leading to the rest of the mall were cordoned off in swaths of rich fabric very reminiscent of the inside of a circus tent.

Elegant. Gorgeous. Unique. Elise couldn't believe Sonya had pulled it off. She'd never doubt her again.

Elise sidestepped the wedding area and ducked behind one of the curtains. Tabitha, Lavina's beautician, was tucked into the first empty store front. The store front's windows and doors were covered with white fabric, but light escaped from the edges. Elise lightly tapped on the door before opening it.

Inside, they'd taken all of Elise's hard work from the night before and finished it into the image of a high-scale salon. There was even a portable sink and a massage chair in the far corner. Two white couches sat casually in the center of the room, along with a coffee table filled with snacks on silver trays.

"Elise!" squealed Catalina from a leather beautician's chair. Tabitha was behind her, looking calm, cool, and just as beautiful as Elise expected any hairdresser of Lavina's to look.

"Happy wedding day!" Elise smiled. She reached into her purse and pulled out a small box. "From me, to you."

"Oh, Elise! You shouldn't have." Catalina's little hands reached out eagerly. She tore off the lid and gasped at what was inside—a tiny blue-enameled balloon charm. "It's adorable!" she squealed.

"Just a little something blue that reminded me of the circus," Elise explained.

"I love it! I'll wear it right here!" Just like that, Catalina tucked it inside her bodice.

They visited for nearly a half an hour and Elise was relieved to see that Catalina's apparent happiness seemed uninfluenced by medication. "Well," Elise said finally, with a glance up at the beautician. "It looks like you're in good hands. I'll check on you in a bit, but otherwise, relax and enjoy."

"Wait, before you go," Catalina beckoned her over. In a low voice, she continued, "Have you seen Cook?"

A feeling of foreboding crept up Elise's spine. "What? No."

"I haven't seen him since the rehearsal." Catalina's bottom lip poked out in a bit of a pout.

"Did he have a bachelor party?" At Catalina's shake of the head, Elise continued, "Maybe he's off doing something special for the honeymoon. I'll keep my eye out for him, but I'm sure everything's fine."

Elise didn't feel as confident as her words as she left for the arboretum.

She felt a bit surprised as she entered. Just in the little while that she'd been gone, the room was transformed by noisy people. She stood silently against the wall and watched the remaining seats fill. What was even more bizarre was the number of guests who'd chosen to dress like clowns. She shivered at all the white faces, and painted lips and eyes. The congregation's chatter was raucous and loud as if fueled by the energy of the costumes.

"There you are," Sonya snapped, walking up to Elise. A long bag draped over her shoulders flapped with the fervor of her steps. "I've been looking everywhere for you."

"I was with Catalina. Have you seen Cook?" Elise asked.

Sonya rolled her eyes and let out a sigh. "Are you kidding me? This is a nightmare. Come with me. Now." She grabbed Elise's arm with a firm grip and half-dragged her behind the curtain to the right that would eventually open to the reception area. "I have got to talk to you," she mumbled.

Sonya looked around, as if searching for a place to speak privately, and finally settled on an empty kiosk. Reaching into her bag, she pulled out a manila envelope and placed it on the counter. Her frown lines deepened around her mouth.

Elise took it in with a flicker of interest. "What's going on?"

Sonya tapped the envelope with her fingers, nails short and blunt. A ring glittered on her index finger. "You'll never guess what came in the mail today," she whispered.

With eyebrows lifted, Elise asked, "Well? What?"

"A letter. Proof that it's all fake."

"What's all fake?" said Elise, feeling the blood drain from her face.

"This whole thing. The wedding. It's a sham. None of it's real." Emotion heightened the last of Sonya's whispered words.

Elise reached for the counter to steady herself, then looked at the papers before Sonya. "How do you know? What does that say?"

"Someone sent me a letter warning me that no real marriage license was filed. That they are grifters with a long line of thievery behind them, and that they are being investigated for robbery."

"Are you kidding?" Elise stammered, her mind spinning. *A fake? The whole thing?* "Is Catalina even pregnant?"

"I just told you that they pulled the wool over our eyes, and all you can think about is if Catalina is really pregnant? We have a disaster on our hands." Sonya's face crumpled with worry.

The piano music carried into the room, signaling the ceremony was about to start. Elise rubbed her arms, unsure of what to do. "Are you confronting them now?"

"Confronting them? How exactly am I supposed to confront them? With an anonymous letter?" Sonya had tears in her eyes. "I'm afraid of spooking them. All I want to do is to make sure their check doesn't bounce. And then, I want them gone and out of my life as soon as possible." Sonya wiped under her eyes and took a deep breath to compose herself. She tucked the paperwork back into her oversized bag and looped the straps over her shoulder like an old-fashioned mailman. "Please don't say anything. Not yet."

"Of course not. What do you want me to do now?" Elise asked, feeling lost.

"I want you to go in there and keep an eye on them. Don't leave their sides. Make sure no funny business happens. In four hours or so, we can wash our hands of this whole affair."

Elise closed her eyes and took in a deep breath. Letting it out slowly, she nodded and headed back to the arboretum.

She walked from behind the curtain and sidled to the back of the room. Her gaze swept over the crowd of people, the colorful wigs of the clowns scattered among the congregation like confetti. How did Catalina and Cook know so many people?

Ahhh. There was Brad sitting in the fifth row. She'd give anything to go jump in his arms right now. She needed to talk to him desperately. If only she could call a giant time out and stop everything.

There's Cook standing up front. Thank heavens. Wait, why am I happy if this is all fake? But he looks absolutely giddy with excitement right now, bouncing on his toes and smiling at his best man. A best man dressed in clown gear.

What is even going on?

Could the letter Sonya received have been a hoax? Someone trying to discredit the carny wedding and snub them like the hair salon had?

The pianist slowly faded off her song and stopped, allowing the silence to build. Elise frowned and crossed her arms. It was too late now. She'd just have to figure it out when everything was said and done. People began shifting in their seats to look toward the back of the room. The photographer stood in the middle of the aisle, with her camera lens focused on the area Catalina would be coming through any minute.

Suspense began building as the hush of the room grew.

With a somber look, the pianist began the bold notes of the wedding march and, with a rustle, everyone stood.

The curtains parted, and Catalina strode serenely through pushing a wheelchair. Her father. The old man was covered in a plaid blanket tucked around his thin body. A black bowler hat, decorated with a huge flower, sat on his head. He honked his red nose and waved at the guests.

Soft laughter sprinkled among the guests, and Elise saw more than a few wipe their eyes.

Elise looked to see Cook flush at the sight of her and wipe his eyes, too. He grinned in the way that made him look both bashful and enraptured as he clasped his hands behind him.

Catalina smiled at her man confidently and started forward, slow and easy. She looked lovely. The long flowing white dress was accentuated at the waist with a green ribbon. Small sprigs of green flowers made a flowery crown on her short blonde hair. The wheelchair didn't make a sound as it rolled along the carpet. Catalina's dress swept up the scattered rose petals sprinkled about.

Once at the front, Catalina bent low to kiss her father and pat his thin hand. Her Uncle Rozzo took control of the chair then and pushed it into a waiting spot in the family's row. Cook stepped down to take Catalina's hand. He drew it up to his lips and kissed it, before murmuring, "You look beautiful."

There was a hush as the audience watched in awe. Even as far away as she was, Elise could hear his words.

Anxiety started to ball up in Elise's chest and she clenched her fists. *Are they that good of actors?* She thought about the robbery at the jewelry store; that was the day she'd first met them. Was that a coincidence they were there?

The thought actually made her feel queasy. She just couldn't do it, couldn't stand there and watch them fake their vows. It was too conflicting. In fact, she was seized with an almost irresistible desire to cry out, "Stop! I protest!" When had they quit including that in the wedding ceremony? Her hands started to sweat as the feeling grew stronger. Watch her single-handedly destroy what they'd worked so hard to make happen.

She had to get out of there.

Chapter 23

Elise hurried through the curtain and passed by the kiosk, wishing she could leave the entire building. *There's nothing more I can do at the ceremony, except to ruin it. I'll just check on how the reception is shaping up.*

She tried to squash her personal feelings, with little success. *Catalina was becoming my friend! She tricked me?*

With determination to act professional, she stomped harder onto the floor making her heels clack. *Not going to do this. Not now.*

The long hall softly glowed with a trail of little lights that the decorators had strung up the night before. The lights led the way to the reception area. The empty store fronts were dark and spooky as she passed. Her reflection wavered from short to tall as it bounced off of the windows and on to the doors. She clutched her purse tighter to her side and stared straight ahead.

Elise walked into the food court and smiled to see that someone had thought to bring in a cotton candy machine after all. The tables she'd worked on so hard the night before looked amazing, transformed by the tablecloths and flickering candles, with more twinkling white lights overhead. A long line of tiny glass elephants—trunk holding tail— stood on the buffet table along with the serving trays. The silver tureens were set up, but empty.

Her skin prickled.

Something wasn't right. It wasn't what was there, but what was missing.

Sounds. The noisy laughter.

"Hello?" she called, her voice echoing. She paused to listen. Nothing. She walked carefully to keep her heels from making noise as she headed around the buffet table and peeked into the Panda restaurant. She pushed the little opening in the counter back on its hinges and quietly walked back there.

Bright overhead fluorescents lit the kitchen area. The tables were covered with more tureens, and several ice chests sat in one corner. But there were no people.

The hair on the back of her neck prickled. She looked toward the back of the room at a large silver door. Licking her lips, she walked slowly to the freezer. Her hand rested just a moment on the metal handle as she pushed it down with all of her weight to swing it open. Icy air rushed out.

She was too late.

A gasp of horror ripped from her throat, and she covered her mouth.

Flopped over the top of the ice-cream wedding cake, chest up, was the cake decorator. He was dressed in a clown costume, and a tube of frosting still dangled in his hand.

She pulled out her cell phone and quickly dialed.

"911…what's your emergency?"

The operator's voice did little to pry Elise from her shock. All she could see was the frosting—pink, green and white—with nonpareils spilling from a bottle into a pile beside the dead body. Resting next to the corpse's foot was a very conspicuous rubber red nose.

"Uhh… there…there's…" Elise stammered. Her ears rang as the blood rushed from her face. Dizzily, she reached for the table to steady herself. She flinched as her fingers dug into more frosting.

"What's your emergency?" The calm voice asked again.

Elise's mouth was dry as she tried to croak out the words. "Something's happened to the cake decorator."

"Can you give me some more details? Is his airway clear?"

"Um, I think he's dead."

"Are you sure he's deceased?" The voice was irritating in its calmness.

Elise took some deep breaths, trying to get a grip on the situation. "Quite sure. He's been shot in the heart."

She rattled off the address of the mall and in shock, she murmured. "I have to go."

"Are you in danger? Is someone there with a gun?"

"I can't talk. I feel...I have to go." She hung up, feeling the room spin around her. She slipped on the icy floor and her phone skittered away.

What am I going to do?

It felt disrespectful to leave the body, but she couldn't stand to see him anymore. She fumbled for her phone and the battery that had popped out.

She clicked the battery back in place and slowly closed the freezer door.

Call Brad. Her inner voice shouted and broke through her shock. She turned the phone on and watched the progress wheel rotate with agonizing slowness. *Hurry! Hurry!* Staring at the screen, she hurried back to the hallway.

Footsteps made her look up.

"Sonya!"

Her boss clutched her bag and hurried over. "What are you doing out here, Elise? Why aren't you watching the wedding like I said?"

"It doesn't matter. We have an emergency. A real emergency. The cake decorator's been shot!"

Sonya's mouth dropped open in shock. "You're not serious."

"Yes! In the freezer!" Elise pointed in the direction of the Panda restaurant with her cell phone.

"I knew something would happen! I told you Rozzo was being a bit too interested in us. I'm so stupid! I should have known! We need to call the police! Now, where is the body?" Sonya looped arms with Elise, her bag thumping hard into Elise's side, and hurried them both into the reception area. "Where is he?"

"He's in there." Elise pointed, feeling shaky and sick.

"Where? You have to take me to him."

"I don't want to see him again," Elise murmured, shaking her head. She turned back at Sonya.

"Take me to him, now." Sonya held a gun. Her face was calm as she gestured to the restaurant and then pointed the barrel back at her. "Go on."

"Sonya…." Elise was shocked.

"Now, Elise." Sonya's voice was low and gentle. "Hands up."

She directed Elise through firm prods of the pistol's barrel in her back. Elise glanced desperately around the kitchen.

"The caterers aren't coming back. I fired them all. Now, open the door."

Swallowing hard, Elise opened the door. The poor cake decorator stared with sightless eyes. She turned around to her boss. "Sonya, please. I won't tell."

"You won't have a chance to tell. Because I'm not leaving any lose ends behind. I've been planning this for the last year and nothing is getting in my way. Now get in there."

Elise took a few steps back. The floor was slippery under her heels. *Just distract and delay her. The police are on their way.*

There was going to be no distracting her. With emotionless eyes, Sonya lifted the pistol. "I wish you had just done your job and listened to me for once.

What did I say about babysitting you?" She gave a half-shrug. "Goodbye, Elise."

"Wait!" Elise shrieked, waving her hands. "Wait just a second. Did you see what he had in his hand?"

Sonya looked suspiciously over to the corpse. "What does he have?"

"It's just in his hand. I was trying to get it out earlier." *If she gets close enough, I'll knock her off balance in those shoes.*

Sonya took a step inside the cooler, needing to duck under the doorway.

Elise watched her totter on her high heels. Her muscles tensed.

"Back up," Sonya directed, waving her gun again. "Now. Until your back touches the wall."

Elise stumbled back until she felt the radiating wave of cold metal behind her.

Sonya watched her for a second, then looked down at the cake decorator's hand. "What are you talking about? It's just frosting."

The temperature burned Elise's eyes. "I just thought I saw…."

Sonya barked a laugh. "Little Elise. You just thought. That was the problem all along. You lived in your own little world and never saw what was really going on around you. Just a little pawn in my plan, like those carnies."

Elise swallowed hard to calm down. "Why don't you tell me?"

"Tell you? I'm not playing this game." She raised the gun and pulled back the hammer.

"Sonya! NO!" Elise screamed and dropped to the ground.

The gun's blast was deafening.

Elise covered her ears with her eyes squeezed tight against the pain. The high-pitch whine ripped through her ears and her head, until it felt like every part of her was exploding. *I've been shot!* She clenched her teeth and groaned.

Someone touched her.

"Baby? Baby! Are you okay?"

Baby?

"Elise! Talk to me!" Hands roughly rolled her over. She opened her eyes to see Brad's sweet face.

Despite herself, tears gathered in her eyes and she smiled weakly. Her plan worked.

Chapter 24

The curtains were parted just enough for Elise to see the moon as she sat in the hospital bed. Not because she'd been shot. No, nothing as cool as that. But she had turned her ankle when she'd fallen, and was now waiting for x-rays to see if she'd broken any bones or not.

Typical. Shot at by a bad guy. Injured by clumsiness.

"Hi, darlin'." Lavina poked her red head around the privacy curtain. "How're you doing?" Her forehead creased in concern. She gently sat on the edge of the bed. "I passed your man in the hall and he said you were up for a visit."

"Yeah. He had to head back to the station to finish his paperwork on the arrest. I'm fine. Feel kind of ridiculous sitting here with a bum ankle. What's going on out there?"

"The news stations are having a hay day. Oh my gosh. Every John, Jeff, and Sally is out there asking questions about who broke open the great Craigslist case. And wouldn't you know, it would be my best friend." Lavina's green eyes grew misty. "Darn it. You did it again. You promised."

"I swear I didn't mean to get into any danger, Vi. For crying out loud. I worked for a wedding planner. How much safer can it get?"

"Not safe enough. What are you, a killer magnet?"

Elise groaned and flopped her head back on the paper-covered pillow. She sighed and then looked gratefully at her friend. "Thank you for coming."

"Of course. I wouldn't miss it for the world." Lavina entwined her fingers and sat up primly. "Now tell me everything that happened. Did you ever suspect her?"

"Never! But something triggered inside me when I saw her heading down the hall. She was coming from the part we weren't using. She'd been carrying this huge bag all through the preparations for the wedding, and suddenly the bag was full. I knew the only thing down there was a jewelry store."

"Why did you go with her then? To go find the body. Why didn't you just scream?"

"Scream? I don't know. I was pretty much in shock and didn't exactly trust my emotions at the time. She was a friend, and I had a dead body on my hands, so I needed a friend. Besides, I wasn't sure if I was going on overdrive after all my suspicion on Catalina and Cook."

"How in the world did Brad end up there in the nick of time?"

Elise smiled. "You can never pick on me for having a crap phone again because this baby," she reached for her cell sitting on the hospital table, "is able to dial someone just by pushing the 'one' button."

"Huh?"

"I have Brad set as number one in my contacts. I pushed the button and called him as soon as I saw Sonya's heavy bag. I just held down the button and prayed."

Lavina's mouth dropped. "You didn't."

"Yep."

"What kind of pain medicine are you on? You are so, so lucky. What if he hadn't answered?"

Elise shrugged. "I gambled it all."

Ten minutes later she was wheeled into X-ray, where she was informed that she would be needing surgery to straighten out her fibula. In the next breath, the doctor clapped her on the shoulder. "But aren't you the luckiest. I hear you're claiming the Grandstone reward!"

Chapter 25

A week later Elise sat across from Lavina at the steak house restaurant. Her foot was encased in a cast and her crutches leaned against the wall. She ate her sandwich and used her well-practiced, patient smile with Vi.

"Now, I love you, Elise. You're like a sister to me. And I feel I have the right to speak into your life whether you like it or not. You can't collect kids like you did cats," Lavina said.

"Cat," Elise said, cleaning out under her thumbnail. She gave her unflappable smile to her friend.

"You know what I mean. This is a person. A real live person."

"I get that. Don't you think I do? But it's a person who needs a family. Heck, I could use a family too. And, at this moment, I'm just a temporary guardian."

"How did you find her? Did you put up "found" posters?"

"She's not a puppy, and I saw her at the park again. This time I got her to come home with me." Elise's heart squeezed a little, remembering how cold it was that night. Lucy had come out from under a tree, blue lipped and shivering. Elise had taken her home where she'd covered the teen with blankets and fed her hot soup. They'd talked until the sun rose the next morning.

"A match made in heaven," Lavina said dryly.

"Yes, I think it is. What are you so worried about?"

"Well, just a couple months ago you were living off of ramen noodles and tic-tacs. So, yeah, I have some concerns."

"Is it possible your concerns are more about you than Lucy? Like, now I'm not going to be free to run whenever you want. Free to go on trips and stuff."

Lavina pushed on her arm. "Are you serious? You think I'm that shallow?"

Shallow? Elise's brow furrowed. No, she didn't think her friend was shallow, not in the caring about people way. But she did think Lavina was self-centered when it came to her 'fun time.'

Elise continued, again in her most even-tempered voice. "I know that having the responsibility of a child will really change things. I get that it's a big change, not just for me, but for you too. But she needs me."

"She needs a family."

"Look, like I said, it's just temporary. Maybe for only a couple months. The state said they'd reassess after her mom completes rehab. And hopefully she will."

"You hope?"

Elise sighed. "I don't know what I hope. I just know this girl pulled at my heartstrings." She glanced at Lavina. "She reminds me of you when you were little."

The silence between them grew for a couple beats. Lavina had lost her mom at the age of six, and had been forced to move in with her grandparents. Back then, all Elise had understood was that her best friend—the girl who stood up to the school bus bully and punched him right in the nose when he tried to steal Elise's lunch— was moving two houses down the street. It had seemed like the best thing ever, at the time.

But now she knew better. Understood that there had been a cost paid, and not by Elise, but by Lavina who didn't have her mom to grow up with. Elise didn't understand it then, but she'd seen the effects of it on her friend. The protectiveness, the overly-toughness, at times. Still, Lavina's grandparents had been first rate, and that was what had given her that heads up in life. Without them, who knows where Lavina would have ended up.

Lavina groaned and shook her head. Lines of resignation creased her mouth. "Elise…."

Elise continued. "She doesn't have anyone to help her with her mom in rehab. I want to protect her until she gets her mom back. Things will be tight. Super tight. I get it. But we'll be okay. If worse comes to worst, I still have some jewelry I can pawn. And there's Grandstone's reward money, if they ever pay. Right now, I just want her to know she is valuable and wanted, despite her mother's choices."

"Well," Lavina blew out a big breath, then stood up and dusted off her pants. "I sure love you, Elise. You know I always have your back. I guess that means she needs an Aunty Vi, hmmm? Let's go shopping and get her a few things."

Elise jumped up too, as excitement flew through her. "Are you serious? You'll support me with Lucy?"

"Are you kidding? I'm your wingman in everything. Although, I guess now I'm your wing-aunt." She scowled briefly. "Just don't expect me to babysit."

"Vi, she's fifteen." Elise answered with a snort. "Seriously? You know more about kids than that."

"I don't know anything about kids!" Lavina snapped back. "I just have that one babysitting experience under my belt...."

"Dear Lord. The time you nearly burnt down the church?"

"Who lights candles in a church?" Lavina quibbled. "Besides, I put the fire out."

"Fire extinguisher foam all over the podium."

Lavina raised a painted eyebrow. "So you're saying...?"

"I'm saying that may be the first nativity scene covered in snow ever. Poor baby Jesus was blanketed in it. Kids screaming."

Lavina rolled her eyes. She calmly plucked a thread from her sleeve before turning her brilliant green eyes to Elise. "It was memorable. Those kids all know —"

"Not to let Lavina babysit. Yes, I think I remember the Sunday School director shouting it."

"Stop, drop, and roll." Lavina continued without missing a beat. Then she smiled. "And who got out of babysitting?" She pointed at Elise. "And who ended up stuck with it for the rest of the year?" She laughed. "You smelled like graham crackers every Sunday." Wrinkling her nose, she hesitated. "Are you going to smell like that again?"

"Good grief. Are you kidding? Of course not. That only happened because I had to hold the Cooper twins, who were always covered in crumbs. Lucy will be fine. Like I said, she's fifteen. Self-sufficient, even."

Lavina grabbed her card out of her wallet and set it next to the bill. She looked for the waiter and gave him a wave when he noticed her. "I'll pay for this," she said as the waiter hurried over. "This might be the last treat you get for a while."

The waiter took the card with a smile. Lavina pulled out her compact mirror and her signature red lipstick from her purse. "By the way," she said, lining her lips in glossy red. "Have you talked with Brad about all of this? What does he think? Does that mean he'll become an instant dad?"

At the word "dad" Elise's heart dropped like a stone. Sure, she'd been thinking about how Lucy would impact their relationship, but she never in a million years thought about Brad carrying the name of dad. Never! No way. This is just temporary.

Most likely.

She took a deep breath and stared down at her lap. Her fingernail polish was chipped again. How could she think of taking in a girl when she was so bad at normal "girl" things? Haircuts, manicures....

It's just nail polish. Quit freaking out. "I don't know how much Brad has actually thought of it. I guess we'll need to have a talk."

"You're kidding?" Lavina accepted the card back from the waiter with her face frozen in surprise. "You haven't had that type of talk yet?"

"Just the bare minimum. He's been really focused in wrapping the Craigslist robbers case up."

"How bare?"

"He knows Lucy needs a place to stay."

"Oh my heavens." Lavina shook her head. "If you aren't one of the craziest people I know." She adjusted her thick necklace. "Well, Brad will be getting a big dose of crazy himself, I guess. By the way, whatever happened about the green heel?"

"It was Catalina's."

Lavina's mouth dropped open. "What? Are you serious?"

"That was the hardest clue, but once I figured it out all the rest fell into place. You see, it wasn't long after Catalina hired Sonya to be her wedding planner that Sonya realized that the circus had been in Meadowford, which was the last town of the jewelry store that she'd robbed. When Catalina wore the green shoes for the first consultation, that's when Sonya got the idea."

"What idea?" Lavina swirled her straw in her soda.

"Her plan was to do a final robbery and pin the Craigslist Bandit thing on the circus."

Lavina took a sip of her sweet tea. "Well, don't leave me hanging. Go on!"

Elise sucked in a deep breath as all the words rushed to her mouth like cattle trying to get through a gate. "At the wedding dress fitting, Sonya had been surprised that Catalina had worn flats instead of heels. It made me realize Sonya had always seen Cat in heels before. Sonya even mentioned that day how Cat always wore sparkly heels."

Elise took a drink of her coke to wet her mouth. "And, it was obvious at the wedding that green was Catalina's favorite color. I realized that heel had to be hers. But how did it get in the alley? Was Catalina guilty? I wasn't sure."

"We finally learned the answer a few days ago when Brad told me he'd found the homeless guy in the old car—remember how he'd been watching me? —and brought him in for questioning. The guy calls himself Todd Danger, and said he'd been hired by Sonya. Somehow, Sonya connected with him after he got fired from the circus, and she paid him good money to do a little reconnaissance job. First on the list was to steal Catalina's shoes and plant them in the Grandstone alley, as Sonya continued to set the circus up to take the fall. In his bitterness, he was happy to acquiesce. Especially since the price was right."

Elise shook her head. "The funny thing was that by him stealing Cat's shoes, it only fueled Catalina's hatred of Lucy, because Cat believed it was the teenager who'd taken her heels. Lucy said she'd caught Todd leaving Catalina's room. When he'd stolen the shoes, he'd also planted the painters mask in Cat's room, and Lucy had swiped it, which is what Catalina had really seen her take."

She paused, remembering the teenager shyly sharing the story. "Lucy had hoped to redeem herself in Catalina's eyes to get a job at the circus, and said she'd kept her eye on Todd. She soon discovered Todd was working with Sonya. She'd tried to warn me that Sonya was involved by hanging the painter's mask in the bathroom. Only Lucy didn't completely trust me either, not convinced that I wasn't in on the plan, too."

"Now I, like an idiot, turned around and showed the mask to Sonya. I just had no reason to suspect her of anything. Sonya already had Todd on my trail by then but, after that, she had him keep closer tabs on me."

"And she had him spy on you why?"

"She'd discovered too late that my boyfriend was a cop. She wanted to make sure I didn't cause any trouble."

"Okay, that makes sense." Lavina looked up as the waiter returned with her card and the check. She tucked her card away, continuing, "So the real question of the hour, why did Sonya kill the cake decorator?"

"He'd been her partner. She'd always been the brains behind the operation, searching which store to rob that was in the area of her latest planned wedding, and placing the Craigslist ads. He was the one who did the dirty work. But she was ready to get out of the business and travel the world, and had planned this heist to be her last gig. And, like she told me, she wasn't going to have any loose ends."

Elise lifted her brow. "Sonya continued to build the groundwork for the last robbery, even going so far as to subtly guide Cat to pick the mall. She made a Craigslist ad asking for clowns to be guests at the wedding. When I found him, the cake decorator had been dressed as a clown. Originally, he was supposed to rob the jewelry store and later, blend in with the guests in case an alarm sounded. At the last minute, Sonya decided she didn't need him after all." Elise made a shooting motion with her hand. "She killed him and did the robbery herself, planning to make a clean escape. No loose ends."

"Now, she's in jail, with loads of evidence against her. How did she deal with the jewelry store's alarm?"

"She had some sort of control over the mall's alarm system. It's how she was able to rent several different businesses at once. It turned out there was a silent alarm tripped at the jewelry store that she didn't know about. It didn't matter, because, by then, I'd already found the cake decorator and called the police."

Lavina shook her head, her eyes wide with disbelief.

"And," Elise continued. "Like I said before, when I saw her coming from that direction with her bag full and weighted, my gut told me to call Brad." Elise winked. "And you always told me to listen to my gut."

"You and that darn clunky old phone." Lavina closed her eyes with a flutter. "You are a lucky, lucky girl. Now, tell me. Who was the mysterious waitress you kept searching for?"

Elise laughed. "That just turned out to be a red herring. Uncle Rozzo actually fell in love for the first time in his fifty-three years. The two live together now, at the circus. I hear he's trying to make her the next bearded woman."

Lavina raised her eyebrow and Elise shrugged in response.

"Besides," Elise continued, "weirdly enough, I was already sort of on guard when I saw the white van unloading flowers the day before. I'd seen a bunch around town being used by different businesses, and it had occurred to me what a perfect escape vehicle that was from a crime scene. You just needed a different magnetic business sign to stick on the side."

"Mmm," Lavina nodded. "And, that night of your surgery to fix that darn leg of yours," Lavina pointed in the direction of Elise's ankle. "You kept murmuring about a fake wedding. What was up with that?"

"Oh," Elise blushed. "That was another way Sonya had set up the Petrovitskys...that their wedding was fake. Sonya had been positive that the final nail in their coffin was proof that they hadn't filed for a marriage license, and were just staging the whole thing. But what she didn't know was that after the positive pregnancy test, Cook and Catalina had eloped earlier in Las Vegas. It was all hush-hush because it would be an insult to the Petrovitsky family to not be included in the wedding."

"Married the whole time...." Lavina's heavily made up eyes were wide.

"Yeah. Crazy, huh?

"Paying all that money, for a dead body and a S.W.A.T. team to crash the wedding."

"I guess one day that will be a memory worth talking about." Elise said with a smile. "In more positive news, Catalina said if they have a girl, her name will be Makylah Elise."

"Awww," Lavina said. "That's so sweet." Her phone dinged and she dug it out of her purse to read the text. Putting it away, she said. "Well, darlin', it's time for me to go. Mr. G is here to pick me up." She smiled with her eyebrow raised. "Would you care to meet him?"

Elise's pulse raced at the thought. "Vi! Are you kidding me?"

"Come on. Let's go." Lavina looped her purse across her forearm and stood.

"Finally. I can't even believe it." Elise started, before grabbing her sweater. She shoved her arms in the sleeves, only to have her ring catch a thread on the inside. No matter what she did, she couldn't pull her arm out or push it through. Flopping her sleeve, she tried to free the ring.

Lavina watched with one eyebrow barely raised and sipped from her tea.

Elise hung her head with frustration before yanking her arm out, dragging a long piece of thread with it. She looked at Lavina and held up a finger, "Not a word."

"I'm not saying anything." Lavina smirked. "Nothing to say to my graceful, beautiful friend."

"Well," Elise laughed. "At least one of those is true."

Five minutes later, they exited the restaurant. The breeze was brisk and carried Elise's hair in front of her eyes. She tried to tuck her hair back and nearly lost her left crutch in the effort. In securing the left crutch, she almost lost grasp of the right one, and then her cast foot dotted against the ground. "I freaking hate these convoluted...."

"Tsk, tsk," Lavina said. "Such language. And in front of my beau, too."

"Where is he?" Elise looked around anxiously as she tried to compose her face and look collected.

"Just over there." Lavina indicated the black limousine with the lift of her finger. Together, they headed over. Elise felt like a combination of the Tin

Man and Bambi on ice with the crutches, but she kept her face serene. I'll make a good impression if it kills me.

As they reached the limousine, a chauffeur raced around and opened the back door for Lavina. Gathering her skirt around her, Lavina carefully climbed in. The chauffeur offered his hand to Elise to help balance her. She hopped a bit to adjust so that she could lean into the car after her friend, ready with a big smile.

Instead, she gasped.

Male laughter greeted her. "Hello, Elise. I've heard so much about you."

The End

Thank you for reading The Honeyed Taste of Deception — Check out Elise's latest adventures in The Tempting Taste of Peril.

When the Cuckoo strikes one,
prepare to come undone.
From these pages will crawl
wonders to conquer all.

Elise read the handwritten sign that hung on the front door of the Capture the Magic bookstore, then blinked hard, her hand hesitating on the doorknob.

And so it begins again…